HEARTLESS GOON 5

Ghost

**Lock Down Publications and Ca$h
Presents**
HEARTLESS GOON 5
A Novel by *GHOST*

Lock Down Publications
Po Box 944
Stockbridge, Ga 30281

Visit our website @
www.lockdownpublications.com

Lock Down Publications
Like our page on Facebook: Lock Down Publications @
www.facebook.com/lockdownpublications.ldp
Cover design and layout by: **Dynasty Cover Me**
Book interior design by: **Shawn Walker**
Edited by: **Lashonda Johnson**

Stay Connected with Us!

Text **LOCKDOWN** to 22828 to stay up-to-date with new releases, sneak peaks, contests and more…

Thank you.

Submission Guideline.

Submit the first three chapters of your completed manuscript to <u>ldpsubmissions@gmail.com</u>, subject line: Your book's title. The manuscript must be in a .doc file and sent as an attachment. Document should be in Times New Roman, double spaced and in size 12 font. Also, provide your synopsis and full contact information. If sending multiple submissions, they must each be in a separate email.

Have a story but no way to send it electronically? You can still submit to LDP/Ca$h Presents. Send in the first three chapters, written or typed, of your completed manuscript to:

LDP: Submissions Dept
Po Box 944
Stockbridge, Ga 30281

DO NOT send original manuscript. Must be a duplicate.

Provide your synopsis and a cover letter containing your full contact information.

Thanks for considering LDP and Ca$h Presents.

Dedications:

First of all, this book is dedicated to my Baby Girl 3/10, the love of my life and purpose for everything I do. As long as I'm alive, you'll never want nor NEED for anything. We done went from flipping birds to flipping books. The best is yet to come.

To LDP'S CEO- Ca$h & COO- Shawn:

I would like to thank y'all for this opportunity. The wisdom, motivation, and encouragement that I've received from you two is greatly appreciated.

The grind is real. The loyalty in this family is real. I'm riding with LDP 'til the wheels fall off.

THE GAME IS OURS !

Ghost

Chapter 1

"Tamia, I'm not gon' ask you this shit again. Who did this to your face?" I grabbed her and held her shoulders. She had a black eye and busted lips. Her head looked like she'd been beaten severely. I was pissed off. I didn't give a fuck what I was going through with my baby mother. Wasn't no nigga about to put his hands on her and fuck her up like that. She looked horrible.

She jerked away from me and pushed me out of her battered face. "JaMichael, why you acting like you care about me all of a sudden?" she slurred. She held the towel that had been dipped in ice water to her lips. "You ain't been caring about me this long." She walked over, sat on the couch, grabbed a blunt out of the ashtray, and sparked it.

I came into the living room and looked down at her. "What the fuck are you talking about? Who did this shit to your face, Tamia?"

"After all that shit we went through as kids, JaMichael. After all of the struggling together and holding each other in the freezing cold when both of our electricity and gas were out at home. After all the promises we made to each other and all the love we confessed for and about each other. Why would you go and leave me for some bitch that ain't did nothing but hated on me since I knew her? That bitch had everything handed to her and we struggled together, yet you chose her over me! What's the matter with you, Ghost?" she screamed.

I looked both ways, then down at her. We were in a small, one-bedroom apartment in North Memphis. The neighborhood was predominantly white folks and there was a very low crime rate. I already knew any loud outbursts or screaming like she was doing could potentially cause the police to be called.

"Tamia, I ain't choose nobody over you. Me and Bubbie are figuring things out. She got two of my sons. She been doing the best she can to hold me down since all that shit kicked off with Jahliya. We just grew close over time. I ain't ask for this shit to happen."

She stood up and blew a cloud of smoke into my face. "It's always all about you, JaMichael. All you care about is you. You don't give a fuck about me. You don't really give a fuck about Bubbie or these kids we pushed out for your big-headed ass. All you truly care about is you. You's a selfish bastard and if I was a man, I would kick yo' ass." She sat back on the couch, set her blunt in the ashtray, picked up her phone, and started texting. "You's a bitch, JaMichael. That's all you are and all you'll ever be." She shook her head and kept texting.

I stood there mugging her for a hot minute. That bitch had my mind all fucked up. I couldn't believe she was talking to me like she was. It seemed as if she was losing her mind. "What the fuck is wrong with you?"

She looked me over. "Nigga, you are what's wrong with me. You got my mind all fucked up and shit. You see, I thought you really loved me, JaMichael. I thought it was going to be me and you forever, but now look. Why the fuck would you save me?" She stood back up and stepped into my face. I could smell the liquor on her breath now.

"What the fuck is you talking about, shawty? Save you from what?"

"From Chino. Why would you bring yo' ass way across town to save me from him when you really didn't want to be with me? Hell, if I'd known you didn't want me, I could've stayed with him. But now you kilt him and my best friend - all for what?" she screamed.

I closed the distance between us and covered her mouth with my right hand. "Bitch, stop all that ma'fuckin' hollering before one of these people call the police. What the fuck is wrong with you? Are you stupid or somethin'?"

She broke free of me and backed up. "I loved Chino, Ja-Michael. You didn't have to kill him. You didn't have to take him away from me if you weren't going to be with me. That's not fair and you had no right killing Jessie."

"Bitch, what?" Tamia was tripping. I didn't understand it. How the fuck was she saying I had killed two people that she, in fact, had killed? All I'd done was beat the fuck out of Chino after he called himself trying to pistol-whip Tamia. Jessie, her so-called friend, had Chino's gun. Jessie tried her best to buck me down, but the gun wound up being on safety and apparently, she didn't know how to work it. Tamia got a hold of her, they fought for a short time, and somehow, some way, Jessie, wound up with a knife in her throat. That was before Tamia had taken the gun from Jessie and aired Chino out with it. Yeah, Tamia had to be losing her mind.

"I don't want your baby, JaMichael. I hate that baby and I hate your guts. As far as I'm concerned, that baby ain't gon' do nothing but turn into a rotten, dirty killer like you." She picked up the pillow from the couch and threw it at me.

Suddenly it dawned on me. Since I had been there, I had not seen my son, Taurus. I looked around the room. "Tamia, where the fuck is my son?"

She broke into a fit of laughter. "Aw, now you worried about him?" She waved me off. "Boy, bye."

I rushed that bitch and pinned her ass against the wall. "Where the fuck is my son?"

She closed her eyes and smiled. "This is the most action I done got from yo' ass in weeks. It feels good, too." She exhaled, then slowly opened her eyelids. "Ahhhhh! Ahhhh! Help me—help me, he's trying to kill me!"

I placed my hand over her mouth. "Where the fuck is my son, Tamia?"

She cocked back her leg and kicked me right in the nuts as hard as she could, buckling me. I fell to my knees, then to my side. "That muthafucka better know how to swim." She started cracking up. "I hate you, JaMichael! You killed my friends." She kicked me in the side as I was trying to get up, then she ran and disappeared down the hall, screaming at the top of her lungs.

I struggled to come to my feet. I had to rest against the wall. It felt like my balls were in my stomach and like I had to throw up. When I finally gained my composure, I took off down the hall behind her. When I was two steps inside of the hall, she opened the bathroom door and slung Taurus out of it. I mean she threw him in the air. "Here, take his li'l bitch ass. I hate him, too!"

I don't know how I managed to do it, but as he was floating through the air I tripped over my own fuckin' feet from being caught off-guard by her sheer madness and dove, catching him at the same time my elbows bumped against the gray carpet. He was wet and appeared to not be breathing. His eyes were wide open.

"Ha, ha, po' baby. Fuck him!" She slammed the bathroom door. As soon as it was closed, she opened it and ran into the bedroom.

I laid my son on his back. Tears started coming out of my eyes. "Damn, Taurus, please, man." I tapped his cheek, then lowered my head to his chest to see if I could hear a heartbeat.

Before I could get my ear on it good enough, Tamia ran out of the bedroom naked with a shotgun. I stood right up.

"You finna die, JaMichael. It's time to meet yo' muthafuckin' maker." She pumped it and aimed the barrel at my head. "Say yo' prayers, you silly rabbit." She started cracking up again, then flipped serious.

I held up my hands. "Tamia, what the fuck is wrong with you?"

"Say yo' prayers, Ghost! Say 'em! Say now I lay me down to sleep! Say it—say it—say it, ahhhh!" she hollered.

She aimed the shotgun and placed her finger on the trigger as tears ran down her face. I dropped my head and rushed her as fast as I could.

Boom!

The shotgun went off at the same time the police rushed into the apartment, every bit of twenty deep. They had on masks and tactical equipment. Before I knew it, we were being bum-rushed.

***

Six months later, Bubbie sat across the visiting table from me. She held my hand and wiped her tears with a Kleenex.

"That bitch bogus, daddy. She admitted to Jessie's murder and the attempt on Taurus's life. She still swears you are the one that bodied Chino. How the fuck did she get your gun to be able to turn it into these people?"

I shook my head. "I still don't know, but all they got is her word against mine, right?"

She nodded. "Yeah, and it helped that they found out she was on that PCP real tough. You didn't know she was on that either?"

"Nawl, Chino must've turned her onto that, too. He stayed fuckin' around in D.C." I slammed my fist on the table. "What my lawyer saying?"

Bubbie smiled. "He says you're going to beat this shit. They ain't got nothing on you but her word. They already caught her in more lies than Donald Trump. Cassius Alexander and Shawn Walker dropped a hundred bands for one of the best attorneys in Memphis. You'll meet with him tomorrow. They say they'll be flying out to see you in a month or so and to keep writing that uncut shit with no filter. The streets eating it up., I'm proud of you, daddy."

"This shit coming natural, baby. I can't sleep. I'm up writing all hours of the night like an insomniac. I been through so much shit. But make sure you send my gratitude to both of them and let 'em know I'ma keep doing my thing."

"Will do. Oh, and they sent you a few bands through Access for your commissary. You should be straight for a minute."

"What about you? You got that bag I left?"

She nodded. "Yeah. I didn't know you had so much money put up. Then again, I shouldn't have ever underestimated you to begin with."

"You know that." I tightened my grip on her hand. "Baby, you know I'm finna come from under this, don't you?"

"There is no doubt in my mind that you are. I'ma be right here by your side when you do, ten toes down." She looked into my eyes and exhaled. "Jahliya pregnant. I ain't gon' tell you by who because you gon' flip. Danyelle had the baby. It's a girl, as far as I know. Her mother Veronica said it came out very healthy and beautiful, with hazel eyes like her. She sends her love, and so does Jahliya. They will be out to see you soon. Shemar handled his bidness and Nikki said to tell you that you are free. Just come from under that situation, to let her know what you need, she got you. Shemar says the same. My mother says she knew you weren't nothing but a finer version of my father." She rolled her eyes. "Whatever." She squeezed my hand. "I miss you, daddy. I'm going crazy without you. I can't wait until this is over."

"Hey, hey, hey. You gotta be strong, li'l mama. I got this. I'll be home to my baby girl real soon. Who's my baby girl?"

"Me."

"And who do I love more than anybody else?"

"Me." She wiped her tears away.

Ghost

Chapter 2
JaMichael

"Yo, Ghost, you stupid as hell if you fight this nigga and you finna go home in literally a few hours. You already know dese niggas jealous as a bitch 'cause you made it out these gates, bruh. You need to let this shit go." Rock said this looking over his shoulder, down the row of cells that made up our cell block.

Even though I heard what he was saying, I couldn't really feel what he talkin' 'bout. I was too amped up and ready to bang dis nigga Frenchie. "Nigga, I hear what you sayin', but fuck all of dat. Dis nigga been on my ass wit' dis fuck shit ever since I been in dis ma'fucka. I been ducking his action 'cause I was tryna get my eighty-five percent release, but now that I touch back to the streets in the morning, I gotta have his ass tonight. Dat's just how dat shit finna go right there." I kept grinding my toolie on the concrete floor, checking the blade every now and then just to make sure that it was getting sharper and sharper.

Rock was about 5'6" tall with caramel skin and short dreadlocks. He kept the sides of his head shaved and a big bushy beard like James Harden. I didn't fuck wit' a lot of niggas, but I found the homie to be cool after we'd been forced to be cellmates for a few months. He was from Baltimore, Maryland, and of course I was from Memphis, Tennessee.

"Say, kid still got six years left to do in dis bitch. He ain't got shit to lose, and I heard that the state of Texas just brought a few more serious charges against dis nigga. Dat means dat when he gets up out of here dat he finna have to go through the system all over again with the state of Texas. Yo, dis nigga really fucked up, so fa you to even lower yourself to his level is beyond me, B." He rested his arm on the bars of

17

my cell and kept looking over his shoulder to make sure that nobody would have the opportunity to walk up on me to see what I was doing. Even though he and I hadn't be jamming that long, I could tell that he was a stomp-down nigga like myself. He stayed low, was antisocial like me, and he didn't get caught up in all of the gossip and garbage that took place on the compound. Neither did I. I had spent most of my time writing book after book, so I didn't have time to get caught up in the fuckery no way.

I finished sharpening my toolie and wrapped it into a towel before tucking it into the lower back of my waistband. "Bruh, I don't give a fuck what that nigga finna be faced wit'. Dat shit ain't got nothin' to do wit' me. Like I said before, I been accepting all of his disrespect and bullshit just 'cause I wasn't trying to fuck my programs off. But now that dem bitches is done and my release is in the morning, I gotta see dis nigga bleed one time. You already know how dat shit be." I knew he could because over the past few months, I'd watched the homie stab up a few niggas for one reason or the other. That was another reason I had taken to him. It was because he was about that blood-shedding shit, and he ain't take nothing from nobody. As a killa myself, I could always honor and respect another nigga of my caliber.

"Bruh, you already know how dem Houston niggas get down. They all about jumping a nigga. They don't believe in fair fights. You already know dat I'm not about to let dem jump you, so dat mean dat we about to paint the hallways red wit' dese niggas' blood. You run da risk of fucking off yo' release and getting some extra time. Are you cool wit' dat?"

Before I could even answer his question, I heard Frenchie's voice coming down the gallery where our cells were located. "Ghost, where you at, Memphis-ass nigga? I'm tryna fuck wit' you for a minute," he called.

"Here we go wit' dis shit," Rock said, backing to the side of the opening of my cell. He squeezed his fingers into fists and placed a calm look on his face while he looked in the direction of Frenchie.

I slid my toolie around so that it was on my right hip. That way I could get to it faster if I needed to. He came and stood in the door way of my cell with two of his Texas niggas standing behind him. He had a dumb-ass grin on his face. Frenchie was about six feet even, caramel-skinned, with long braids and a mole on the left side of his cheek.

"Fuck you always got my name in yo' mouth for, nigga?" I snapped at the sight of him.

He laughed. "Word on the street is that you go home in the morning. How true is dat?"

"Dawg, why the fuck you worried about it? Ain't you got a bitch to sweat?" I asked, mugging his goofy ass.

He laughed. "Yeah, but right now, I'm panty checking you."

"What?" I reached to grab that nigga's neck.

His homies pulled him backward and blocked me from getting at his ass. A guard came on to the gallery, and they backed away from my cell and tried to look nonchalant.

The dark-skinned, bald headed, 6'4" guard looked us all over suspiciously. He stared at Frenchie. "Jones, you down here causing trouble?"

"What? Me?" Frenchie looked shocked. "Come on now, boss, you already know I don't get down like dat. I'm just hollering at my potna fo' he leaves in the morning. You already know how us country boys link up."

The guard didn't look like he was buying Frenchie's shit. "Yeah, well, even so. Y'all gotta keep it moving and find your own gallery. If you wanna holler at Mr. Stevens, then you can do that at rec tonight, and not before then. You got five minutes to move around or else I am going to write you up for being in an unassigned area. Five minutes!" He walked away with sweat coming off the top of his head.

Frenchie waited until rounded the corner. He stepped up to the entrance of my cell again. "Say, Ghost, I know you didn't thank you was 'bout to leave up out dis bitch before we knuckle up, did you?" He smiled and then frowned with hatred. "We gotta do this tonight, and I don't give a fuck what you gotta say 'bout it. After rec, my nigga, in the laundry room. We gon' get it up and that's gon' be dat."

I tried my best to keep my cool. "Say, nigga, we ain't gotta wait until later. We can handle dis shit right now. Fuck you talking 'bout?" I moved one of his guys from the entrance of my cell so that he and I were face to face. My first thought was to buss straight in his shit. I could feel my adrenaline surging within me.

He stood with his arms crossed, calm and collected. "Let me know when I'm supposed to be spooked, my nigga." He grunted and looked over to Rock. He turned back to me. "You talking all dat shit, but we gon' see what it is tonight. You can bring yo' homeboy too. Dat nigga ain't on shit either."

"So y'all don't think fat meat is greasy, huh?" The guard came back on to the gallery with a mug on his face. "Get the fuck off of this tier and back to your cell houses. Now!" he boomed.

"Tonight, my nigga. I'll beat you there," Frenchie said while eyeing me.

"Yeah, awright, nigga, I'll be there," I returned, feeling like I wanted to rush his ass and stab my blade into his neck. My whole life I hadn't ever wanted to kill a nigga as bad as I did him.

The guard followed them until they were off of my tier and out of the building. After they left, Rock stepped into our cell and sat on the gray plastic chair that was in front of his desk.

"Yo, kid, I'm telling you, you need to leave dat nigga alone. Son has an agenda. He trying to fuck yo' shit off. Everybody in here sees how you move. They know you got hella books out there in the game, and they know yo' chips stacked up like Pringles. Dat nigga been hating on you since day one."

"And I've been giving his ass passes ever since then too. I can't even sleep at night imagining how I've been letting him skate on as much shit as I have. I gotta fuck him over, Rock. It's something in me that just can't let that shit slide."

Rock shook his head and lowered it between his legs. "Kid, you already know that I'm fuckin' wit' you the long way. If dis is what you wanna do, den fuck it. I'm wit'chu. Let me get my toolie ready too. I already know it's finna go down."

"Nawl, my nigga, I don't even want you involved. Ain't no telling how these weak-ass niggas finna move. I can't have them coming at you after I leave, 'cause I won't have no way to assist you then. That ain't fair, so fall back."

"You got me fucked up." He stood up. "Me and you been jamming the long way ever since you came through dis bitch. You done had my back, and I done had yours. That's how it's gon' be until the day you bounce. Besides all dat, ain't no hoe in me. A part of me wanna catch dat nigga slipping before he even make it to the laundry room tonight." He rubbed his chin and nodded his head. You forget we work the same hallway detail on the east end, and ain't no cameras around there, especially not in the ventilation ducts where they paying us to vacuum every night before rec. Yeah, I think I might have to squash dis shit before it even gets that far."

I looked him over closely, and I could see that he was serious. I started to think about the benefit of not having to risk killing Frenchie, and all types of ideas got to going through my mind. On the one hand I wanted to whoop that nigga just to prove to him that shit wasn't sweet, but then on the other hand, I knew that it wouldn't end there. After I whooped him, I would have to fight one of his niggas, and after I banged him, another would surface. Before I knew it, I would be using a blade and running the risk of catching a new case. I didn't need nor did I want that. My only option was to have Rock handle that business.

"Say, JaMichael, you already know I'm fucked up in here. I got a year left and no family. If I handle dis nigga tonight, what number we talking 'bout?" he asked, walking into my face.

"Shid, name yo' price."

"Fifteen G's. Fifteen G's and I'll slump dat nigga. They gon' lock us down, but I don't care. You'll still go home, and I'll lay low until the heat dies down. What do you say?"

"Shid, let me get on the phone and holler at Bubbie before I can confirm that amount. Once I know it's good, I'll give you the go ahead. How does that sound?"

Rock held up one finger. He slipped from the cell, and two minutes came back and handed me a phone. "Huh, do what you gotta do." He left the room to get on security.

***

Bubbie picked up after I called her five times and she'd hung up. "Who the fuck is this steady calling me?" she snapped into the phone.

"Shawty, calm yo' li'l ass down, it's daddy. Why you hang up five times on me?"

"Why you ain't text me and just say that it was you calling all along? You know I don't answer the phone from numbers I don't know."

"Anyway, look, dis the move. It's dis fuck nigga here that's trying to trick my shit off. He wanna box tonight. I already know that if I whoop this nigga that it won't end there. If it don't end there, then there is going to be a bunch of bloodshed, and there is a chance that I won't be able to come home tomorrow."

"Aw, hell nawl, I been waiting on you for over five years and you thank I'm about to let you fuck dis off at the end? You gotta be crazy. Stay in yo' cell and play pussy until they let you up out of there tomorrow. Damn, you ain't always gotta be a Billy bad ass."

"Will you shut up and let me finish? Damn." I looked around to make sure that nobody was paying attention to me crouched down on the side of my bed with the phone to my ear. From as far as I could tell they weren't, so I went back to my conversation.

She smacked her lips. "Gon' 'head."

"Anyway, you already know how I get down. I want my nigga to ice this fuck boy, and I wanna hit his ass wit' a few bands to make it happen. Ain't shit gon' come back to me. I'll be able to lean back and chill until they let me out in the morning. Cool?"

"JaMichael, as long as you're going to be out the way, and you don't have nothing to do with what they're getting ready to do, I'm good wit' it. Do what you gotta do. We'll go from there. Awright?"

"Dat's all I needed to hear. I love you, and I'll see you in the morning."

"I love you, and I hope to see you there too. Later, daddy."

"Later boo."

When Rock came back into the room, I handed him back his phone and gave him a thumbs up. He nodded his head and disappeared with the phone. When he came back, he grabbed his work clothes for his janitorial job and hugged me. There were no words exchanged. He disappeared, and I laid back on my bunk after grabbing a big bag of Flamin' Hot Cheetos. I got to crunching loud as hell with a smile on my face.

***

That night, I showed up to the laundry room ready to handle Frenchie if I needed to. I stood there with my gray gloves from the prison catalog on my hands and my toolie tucked into my lower back. Five of Frenchie's homeboys were already present. I didn't pay them any mind. Instead, I stood my ground in front of the huge washing machines that were used to wash large amounts of clothes at one time, silent.

After standing there for ten minutes, Rock slipped into the room and gave me a head nod. I noticed that he'd switched shirts, and there was a slight scratch on his face. He looked off and mugged every man in the room.

"Fuck dis nigga at, man? Damn, we only got five minutes before the jakes come through to check this area," I said, looking around at his homeboys.

They remained silent. They stood with their hands tucked under their arms. I could tell that they were confused as to why Frenchie hadn't shown. But like I said, they remained silent until another four minutes had passed.

Rock stepped forward. "Clearly da homie been stood up. Dat nigga is a no show. Fuck it, we gotta move before Sergeant Moore come through this bitch and hand out a bunch of sanctions. I'm out."

"Me too."

And because I left, the Texas niggas did too.

That night, the count was stalled for two hours. They locked down the joint until they found Frenchie on the boiler room floor, stabbed over twenty-five times. At his discovery, they kept the joint locked down. I didn't give no fucks. The joint being locked down for the remainder of the night meant that I didn't have to worry about a nigga doing nothing to me. Though we were stationed in a Minnesota federal prison, ninety-five percent of the population was from all over the United States outside of Minnesota. And in my opinion, the majority of those niggas were haters to the third degree. I couldn't wait to leave they sucka asses.

Ghost

Chapter 3

"Yo, Ghost, don't forget about me, nigga. I did what I had to do with no hesitation. I'ma need you while I'm in here. Nigga, make sure I'm straight. That's all I ask." Rock said this before he pulled me close and gave me a half hug.

"I got you, Blood, you know that." I hugged him, and then backed up. "Dawg, hold ya head in dis bitch. All you got is a year left. That's light. Knock dat shit out and come on home. I'ma make sure I got a bag waiting for you. Dat's my word."

"That's bond den, kid." He broke our embrace and stepped backward, sitting on the bunk. "Keep ya head up. I'ma hit you up later. When can I expect that cheese?"

"Soon as possible. I got you," I swore.

The guard came to the cell and closed it, separating Rock and myself. "Awright, Mr. Stevens, it's time for you to leave the institution. The sooner we get you out of here, the sooner I can sit back on my ass. You sho' you don't know what happened to Frenchie Taylor last night, or who did it?"

"Who?" I looked him over as if he'd spoken a foreign language.

"Yeah, I thought so. Let's go."

"Don't forget about me, JaMichael. Yo' word should be bond, bruh."

I nodded. "Can't be shit but that."

I continued to walk down the gallery while the other niggas stood at their bars with their arms out of them. They mugged me and mumbled incoherent things all under their breaths. I ignored them and kept it moving. It was my moment. I'd knocked down five long years, and for me, it was time to get back to the money. I could already smell the blue faces that were calling out to me.

***

The guards led me down a bunch of corridors, and eventually out of the prison. I wound up at the gatehouse, where I got fitted in the black, purple, and gold Supreme fit that Bubbie had waiting on me with the 2020 Laker Championship Lebrons. They offset my 'fit perfectly and made me feel like a boss. She had two gold chains for me, a pair of Chanel gold frames, and a pair of two carat diamond earrings with a gold Patek, not to mention my underclothes that were all Chanel. I got right, and couldn't help nodding my head with a big, dimpled smile on my face. "Yeah, it's time to get up out dis bitch. Let's get it."

***

When I stepped outside of the big blue metal door of the institution, the sunlight shined down on my forehead and heated it immediately. I pushed the shades back on my face and shook my wrist to see how the sun was gon' play with the gold of the Patek. Yeah, I liked the sight of that. We made it to the final gate that was right by the parking lot, and when I looked to my right, I saw Bubbie standing in front of a cherry red Range Rover with red and black rims on it. She started jumping up and down from afar, then she took off running toward the gate, leaving behind what looked like my sons, but I couldn't quite make them out just yet.

I got geeked up at her enthusiasm. "Yeah, there goes my baby right there. Let me up out this bitch so I can hug my shawty."

The guard ignored me. He stepped up to the gate and waved his hand to the tower officer. The tower officer nodded at him. The next thing I knew the gate was opening and my heart had dropped in my chest. I felt breathless.

"Well, Mr. Stevens, you're a free man. Here." He handed me a Coronavirus mask. "Before you step through that gate, you must have this across your face."

Bubbie hurried to the gate. "Uh-uh, he doesn't need that. I got him this one." She held up a Supreme Coronavirus mask that matched my clothes. She herself had on a Fendi mask that offset her eyes.

"I'm sorry, ma'am, but protocol is protocol." The guard held the mask up higher for me to take a hold of.

"Really, bruh? My shawty right there. I can grab that mask and put it on right now, and you mean to tell me that you finna make a big deal of dis shit?" I asked, irritated.

"Rules are rules." He held it up higher. Sweat slid down his red face. His bald head was already sunburnt.

"Baby, forget it, just grab the mask and let's keep it moving," Bubbie ordered.

"Man, I'm so glad this shit over." I grabbed the mask from him and placed it over my face. "Can I go now?"

"Yes sir, now you can. Don't come back." He nudged me forward.

After I got into the parking lot, he slammed the gate so loud that it made my ears ring. I guess it was his way of reminding me of where I had come from, and where I could wind back up if I slipped.

Bubbie rushed me and jumped into my arms just as I was throwing the bogus mask to the ground. "Daddy home! Daddy home!" she hollered, wrapping her arms and legs around me. "Daddy, I missed you so much. Damn, it's fucked up out here."

I twirled her in a circle and kept her securely in my arms. "I missed you too, baby. Because of the Coronavirus pandemic, she and I had not been able to see each other physically for our visits for fourteen months, so we were reduced to Zooming and praying to God that we were able to remain strong on both ends. Luckily we were. I was thankful for her and her strength. She had held me down for five long years like a champion. I had to make sure that I spoiled the fuck out of her.

I put her down and looked her over. She'd gained about ten pounds from the last time I'd seen her physically, and it looked good on her. Because of our distance, she always struggled with maintaining a healthy diet. Some days she would have an appetite, and other days she wouldn't. So to see the little weight sticking to her body was a blessing to me. She looked so gorgeous with her yellow and purple Fendi skirt dress that clung to her every curve. Her ass poked out from her back, and her thighs had gotten juicy as well. Her hair was natural and appeared all over her head, but neatly. She had a Fendi hair clip that slicked her thick, curly hair back just enough so that it didn't fall into her face.

"Baby, look at you. You look good as hell, girl."

"You thank so? Even after having yo' big headed ass three kids?" She turned in a circle and held her arms out at her sides.

I looked her up and down and without a doubt, she got my stamp of approval. Bubbie was still killing the game in my opinion. Even her toes were done up with a French pedicure with the Fendi logo all over them. I was a pure sucker for a female with pretty toes, especially hers. "Yeah baby, you killing shit. Damn, I missed you." I pulled her to me and tongued her ass down while I rubbed all over her booty. It had gotten bigger as well, and softer. My fingers cuffed it, and I groaned into her neck. "You already know I'm finna tear this ass up tonight."

She laughed. "You think so?"

"I know so." I pulled her to me again and licked all over her juicy lips. Then I was sucking all over them and cuffing her ass even tighter.

KaMichael ran up and stopped in his tracks. "Eww, Daddy got his hands all over Mama booty. That's gross."

LaMichael, my other twin, covered his eyes and joined his brother in saying, "Ewww."

Bubbie broke away from me. "Boy, y'all shut up and hug yo' daddy. Don't start acting all crazy and stuff." She pushed them toward me.

"Come here." I picked them up one at a time, and kissed all over their cheeks. Both boys had deep dimples and were extremely handsome. The only way you could tell them apart was because KaMichael had two deep dimples, one on each cheek, and LaMichael only had a dimple on his left side. Both had long braids and were caramel like myself and Bubbie, and both were very muscular already like myself. "Y'all missed Daddy, huh? Did y'all miss me?" I kept kissing all over them while they laughed and tried to get out of my embrace. Finally I put them down and they ran full speed to the car.

Bubbie walked up to me and took a hold of my hands. "Baby, I want you to have a great release day today. I don't want you to worry about anything. I already know how you are. Just chill today and tomorrow we can get on business. Do you understand me?"

I nodded. "Dat's cool. I mean, I'll try. But the way you talking, you already got me nervous. What's the matter?"

Bubbie popped my shoulder. "Daddy, I just said that I don't want you worrying about anything today. We can get into everything that we need tomorrow." She grabbed my hand and led me towed the Range Rover. Now come on, you gotta wake Jahmya up."

I followed her to the truck with my mind reeling. Trying hard as I might, I could not take my mind off of the fact that I knew something was wrong, and I couldn't quite put my finger on it. But I didn't let on how I was feeling. Instead, I got to the truck and opened the back door. There, sleeping inside of her booster seat, was my four-year-old daughter Jahmya. She had on the same kind of dress as her mother, and her natural hair was just as wild. Her diamond earrings sparkled in the sunlight and I melted. I unhooked her and picked her up. "Baby girl, wake up." I kissed her cheeks over and over again until her eyes opened.

She frowned at first. It took her a moment to recognize who I was, and when she did, she reached on for me and started to cry. "Daddy! My daddy! I love my daddy." Her little arms wrapped around my neck, and my knees went weak.

"Ohhh, baby." I patted her little back, and bounced up and down as if she were a newborn instead of a four-year-old. "I love you wit' all my heart, li'l mama, and I been missing you so much." I kissed her jaws and held her close to my heart."

She hugged me tighter and tighter. "Daddy, please don't go back to jail. I love you too much. Plus Mommy was sad and me too." She rose in my arms and laid her cheek against mine.

Bubbie slipped beside me. "Dat li'l girl love you more than anything in this world. Now that you're home, you better do right by dis family. It ain't just 'bout me and you no more. It's about the family. Come on, let's get this show on the road. We got a long drive ahead of us. Memphis, here we come."

***

We weren't more than an hour from the prison when Bubbie got to bringing me up to speed. "Look, JaMichael, I know I said that I didn't want you to worry about nothing, but I might as well let you know what it is, since we can't do nothing but drive anyway. So this is what's taken place in old run down-ass Memphis.

She switched lanes and adjusted the steering wheel just a bit. She grabbed her cup out of the holder and sipped from the straw. She checked her rearview mirror and kept rolling.

"Damn, you doing a lot of shit without saying anything. Tell me what's good," I said, eyeing the side of her head.

"Oooh, Daddy said a bad word." LaMichael squealed, hitting the back of Bubbie's seat.

"So what? He's Daddy. He can say whatever he wants. Right, Daddy?" KaMichael asked.

"Nope," Bubbie cut in. "He doesn't need to be using curse words around y'all. I'ma need you to master your tongue around these kids, JaMichael. "

"Damn, that's my fault." I covered my mouth and laughed a li'l bit. I had been locked up so long that a part of me had forgotten how to talk any different than foul. But she was right. I had to watch my tongue. "Anyway, what's good with the city?"

"Well, first of all, Phoenix and his Duffle Bag Cartel crew took back over the Mound. Most of the Heartless Goon dudes that were rolling under you switched over to him after you left. They got a crazy stranglehold on all of the projects and the surrounding areas. Ever since you been gone, they have been honoring Phoenix as a king. I ain't gon' lie, he eating."

"Yeah, dat nigga eating so much that he couldn't hit my books on a regular basis or make sure my shawties were good.

You already know I'm finna holla at that nigga immediately. Second to that, I gotta have the Mound back."

Bubbie mugged me. "What?"

"You heard what I said."

"JaMichael, don't play wit' me. You ain't about to get out and jump back in the dope game. You're about to finesse your writing and your books. You got some crazy talent that we need to focus on. I thought we were about to jump off into the movies and all of that type of stuff."

"We are." I rolled down the window and placed my arm on the sill of it so I could feel the fresh, free air blowing on my face. "But before we reach that point, our chips gotta be right. Anyway, what else?"

"Mama, tell him about our cousin Kool Aid!" LaMichael hollered.

I looked back at him, and then her from the corners of my eyes. "Kool Aid? What is he talking about?"

She mugged our son from the rearview mirror. "I was going to get to that. But clearly when you have kids, they like popping off at the mouth before you ever get a chance." She sighed.

"Miss me wit' all of dat. Who is Kool Aid, and why is this the first time I'm hearing about dis nigga?"

"Look, I don't feel like getting into all of that in front of the kids. When we get back to Memphis, I'll explain all of that, but for now, let me update you with everythang else."

She started to give me the whole rundown of the city hood for hood until it all came back to the epicenter being Orange Mound. I half listened. I was mostly focused on the fact that my son had blurted out another nigga's name and Bubbie acted like she wanted to take her time explaining who he was. Warning signals went off in my head, and I immediately got to imagining another nigga fucking my bitch, and I felt a way.

To mask this, I kept letting her talk, and before I knew it, we had arrived in Memphis.

Ghost

Chapter 4

It was two in the morning when we got there, and for some reason, I was wide awake. I helped Bubbie put the kids to bed, watched her pray over them, and then we headed upstairs to our bedroom that was mostly cluttered with her stuff. When I walked into the bedroom she was sitting on the edge of the bed talking her jewelry off.

I came and stood in front of her in silence. "Yo, you was fucking another nigga while I was on lock?"

"What? Boy, nawl. What would make you ask me some goofy shit like that?"

I pulled my shirt off and tossed it on the bed. I stood before her heavily tatted and muscled up from pulling a five year stint. "Cause our son hollering dis Kool Aid nigga. Who the fuck is that? And don't give me that cousin shit 'cause I already know that ain't what's the real."

Bubbie got up and shook her head. "Yo' first day out. Instead of you trying to ball me up and fuck me crazy, you really wanna take this route, huh?" She placed her jewelry into a jewelry box and closed it. "For your information, Kool Aid is your cousin. You had an uncle by the name of Juice. He was your father's brother. Kool Aid is his blood son. About three years after you got locked up, he moved up from New Orleans. He found Jahliyah first, and then Jahliyah led him to us. I was gon' tell you about him, but you blow every fuckin' thang out of proportion, so I was just gon' wait until you got home so you could meet him yourself. But of course, the kids wouldn't allow for that to happen."

I ran my tongue across my teeth. "Dat nigga been up in dis ma'fucka'? Huh? Keep dat shit one hunnit."

"Yeah. That's your cousin, why not?" She frowned and started to take off her clothes before heading for the bathroom to run the shower. After running it, she came back into the bedroom and picked out a red see-through negligée. "Why you still standing there looking like your head is about to explode?"

I had my eyes pinned to a certain spot on the carpet. My jealousy and temper were getting the better of me. "Shawty, what I tell you 'bout letting another nigga walk past the threshold of our home? Huh?"

"But JaMichael, he's your cousin. Who cares?"

"Bitch, I do." I grabbed her ass by the neck and slammed her against the wall so fast that I didn't even know what I was doing until it was done.

Bubbie looked shocked. She remained in place for a second with her eyes bucked wide open. Then they lowered, and she pushed out at me as hard as she could. "Nigga, have you lost your rabbit-ass mind." She swung and slapped my face sideways.

I released her for a second, and then grabbed her neck again, choking the shit out of her. "Bitch, you think shit sweet, don't you? You done had some other nigga in my shit while I was pulling a stint in the bing. Fuck type of female is you?" I lifted her into the air and tossed her on the bed.

She bounced on it twice before rolling off of it. She wound up on the carpet. She jumped up and rushed me at full speed. "You said you never gon' put yo' hands on me, JaMichael! You already doing this shit on yo' first day out. I'm finna break yo' neck!" She ran, swinging her arms wildly.

I was fresh from the joint. While locked, I'd gotten in no less than two fights a week for the last three years straight. So when she swung her li'l fists, blocking them came natural. I knocked her out of the way and tackled her to the bed. Once there, I straddled her and held her down. I scooted lower just a bit until I was between those thick-ass thighs. "You been letting a nigga fuck while I was gone? Huh?"

"Get off of me! I hate your stupid ass! How the fuck is you coming at me like this?"

I leaned my body weight on her small frame and felt between her thighs. Her panties were flimsy, pink and lace. I slipped my right hand into them and over her juicy trimmed pussy. My fingers searched, looking for her opening. "Answer me!"

She twisted her hips right and left trying her best to get me off of her. "JaMichael, get off of me. I ain't feeling you right now. You're talking this dumb shit."

I wasn't trying to hear that. I knew that Bubbie was mad, and I knew that whenever I made her mad that she wasn't trying to fuck until I got her emotions back in check. Seeing as this was my first day out and I wanted some pussy right then and there, I didn't feel like going through the long process of getting her back right emotionally, and I honestly didn't want to know the real answer of if she was fucking with anybody since I'd been locked up. I didn't think I could handle that knowledge at the moment. What I wanted to do was take her ass down, and that's what I was about to do. I didn't give a fuck if she wanted to or not.

"Get off of me! JaMichael!"

I ripped her panties all the way off and threw them to the floor. Then I tore her bra down the middle. Her breasts spilled out. They were bigger than the last time I had seen them. They sagged just a bit, and I liked the natural look and feel of them. "Damn, boo, yo' li'l ass done got so sexy." I held her wrists and ran my tongue in circles all around her nipples until they turned hard. Then I pulled them with my lips and licked all over the nipples again.

She moaned and her thighs fell open. "I hate you, JaMichael."

I wasn't trying to hear that. I licked down her neck and released her hands. My teeth dug into the skin of her neck. I pulled and sucked. She shuddered, and once again her thighs opened up. My hand rubbed her pussy lips in a circular motion. She grew wet. I separated her folds and sank down on her body. "You cheated on me?"

"No! Stop saying that stupid ass shit. You already know I would never cheat on you, especially not wit' yo' cousin."

I kissed her pussy and sucked the juicy lips into my mouth. One thing about Bubbie, was that she'd always had real thick pussy lips. The hornier she became, the thicker they got. Well, they were so swollen at this time that they looked like they were getting ready to pop. I got to sucking and licking all over them hungrily, slobbering, and making all kinds of nasty noises that had her with her back arched and her ankles around my head. She forced me further into her gap and started to ride my face with her hips in a round and round motion.

"Unnnh! Unnnn! JaMichael! I hate you, daddy!"

I pressed her right knee to her chest and started to finger her pussy at full speed with two digits while I sucked on her clitoris. My tongue flicked her nub from side to side. She screamed and tightened her thighs even more around my neck. Then she began to squirt against my lips, and shiver uncontrollably. I sucked hard on her pearl then.

"JaMichael! JaMichaelllllllllll! Awwwww fuck, daddy!" She threw her head back and fell to the bed, jerking up into the air.

I climbed from under her and walked across the bed with my knees after I stripped off my clothes. My dick was already up and hard as the economy. I pumped it and took a hold of her hair. "Come on, boo, give me some of that boss before I wear that ass out."

She turned her head. "No. I'm mad at you."

"Bubbie, stop playin' wit' me, shawty, and suck daddy up. Come on." I tried to force her to look my way so I could guide my piece into her mouth. "Huh."

"No. I ain't fucking with you tonight. You probably really do think I cheated on yo' ass while you were gone. Do you have any idea how that makes me feel?"

I frowned. "Yo, I ain't about to get into your emotions right now. Fuck that. Come here" I grabbed her waist and pulled her back to me. I got between her thighs with her fighting me every step of the way. I held my piece, stroking it over and over. My head found her split, and I weaseled my dick into her crease of heat. "C'mere, boo."

"No." She tried to kick out at me.

I caught the back of her thighs and forced them to her ribs. Her pussy busted wide open. As soon as it did, I slid in deeply. My head traveled through her heat. Her cave was tight and wet. I groaned and bit into her calf muscle. It had been so long. "Shit, baby."

She closed her eyes and opened her mouth wide. Her tongue hung out of the side of it. A bit of drool dared to slide down her cheek. She jerked and turned her head sideways.

I pulled all the way back and slammed forward. "Huh!"

"Unh! Daddy!"

"Nawl, fuck that. Gimme this pussy." I turned into a complete animal, pressing her knees to her titties and long stroking her for all she was worth.

"Unh! Unh! Unh! Unh!" She arched her back and humped into me harder and faster. Her breathing became ragged. She kicked out her legs and held them out as if she was trying to hit the splits while I fucked her as hard as I could, loving the feel of her tight box. "Fuck me, daddy! Fuck me! Unnnn! Shit. Fuck me! Oooh!"

I didn't need her motivation to do what I needed to do. Every stroke was harder than the last one. I reached as deep as I could, searching for the angle of her G spot, and got to hitting it so hard that she fell back once again and started to gasp loudly. Her eyelids were closed tightly. Her nipples were harder than I ever remembered them being. She sat up and licked my face before she came all over me again. The feeling of her shaking and squeezing me down low was enough to trigger my own climax. I pushed her knees as hard as I could to her chest and came deep within her womb, over and over again, before falling beside her with my piece twitching in the air like crazy.

She laid on her back for a moment, breathing hard. Then she turned to her side and took a hold of my dick. "I know I owe you dis, JaMichael." She sucked me into her mouth and proceeded to bob her head up and down in my lap over and over, slurping and moaning all around him.

I laid back like a boss. It was feeling so good that from time to time I would groan and tighten my fingers in her hair after I placed them there. I couldn't get the image of another nigga fucking with Bubbie while I was away on lock. I couldn't really say for certain if I truly believed that she would have actually allowed for another man to get between her legs, but then again, I didn't trust or believe nobody. Just by judging her character, I couldn't honesty tell, but at the same time, it was a double standard because I knew damn well that I wouldn't have been strong enough to abstain from pussy for five years or until I was able to fuck her again. That would have been an impossible task. And it's not that I wouldn't have held her down because I would have done that with no problem. But not fucking would have been hard. I loved pussy, *new* pussy way too much, as much as I hated to admit that I had to be uncut with myself.

She got to sucking me as fast as she could while her fist pumped me over and over. Then she took her hand away and solely used her mouth. Her neck went into overdrive. She held my thighs and arched her ass into the air. Her pussy drooled her excitement. I smacked that ass and slipped two fingers back into her while she sent me into overdrive. I felt her teeth softly nip at my head, and it was too much.

"Huh! Huh! Huh! I'm cumming, boo, fuck, here daddy cum again." I humped into her mouth and forced her to swallow me while I bussed back to back, jerking like crazy.

***

That night, I laid in bed with my eyes wide open, holding Bubbie close to my body. No matter how hard I tried, I could not get to sleep. I kept seeing all kinds of weird images in my head of her and another nigga doing the most. I hated myself for having a sucka attack. How could any man expect for a woman to be faithful to him for so many years when he knew for a fact that sexually, he couldn't have done the same thing? That shit was nuts to me. But if one thing was for sure, that was that men were all about double standards. We could fuck another bitch and have it not mean nothing, but if our women fucked another dude we would not only feel betrayed, but as if we needed to kill something. That was the most prevalent one for me. Even though Bubbie was swearing she'd been one hunnit, I couldn't see it, and that shit was making me feel a way about everything.

Ghost

Chapter 5

The next day, I woke up to Jahmya climbing all over me. She crawled across my stomach and laid with her face against mine. Her little arms wrapped around my neck. I opened my eyes to see her as such, and I couldn't help feeling weak. She kissed my cheek and laid her face back to mine.

Bubbie stood over the bed with a phone recording us. "Dang, one thing I can say for sure, that's that this li'l baby is a Daddy's girl. It looks like she coming for my slot." She kept recording.

I hugged Jahmya. Then I picked her up into the air and looked into her pretty slender face. She was so beautiful. She reminded me of my father's mother, and my own. She had deep dimples on each cheek and almond-shaped eyes. Her complexion was light caramel, and her eyes were a honey brown, just like my own. "Hey, li'l mama. How are you doing this morning?"

She smiled and reached her arms out, I guess for me to bring her closer. "I want huggies, Daddy."

I hugged her back to me and kissed her forehead. "I love you, baby."

"I love you too, Daddy. I don't want you to leave any more. I wanna go." Her bottom lip quivered.

"Awwwww, social media about to eat dis up right here. This gon' make all of those broads have Daddy issues. Gon' head on, JaMichael."

I got irritated. "Bubbie, you already know that one of the rules of my federal probation is that I can't be on social media for the first twelve months prior to my release. You gon' get me revoked already, damn." Jahmya hugged me tighter.

"Dang, I forgot all about that." She seemed to be recording for a while longer, and then took the phone away. She looked it over and got to taking what felt like a million pictures of me and Jahmya. When she finished, she sat on the edge of the bed, and kissed my lips. "I'm so happy that you're home, baby. I swear seeing you in the mornings is going to make me so happy every single day." She climbed into the bed and readjusted Jahmya so she could place her in my arm on the opposite side of where she wanted to lay her head on my chest.

I laid there with my girls, feeling like a champion. Jahmya fell asleep with her cheek against mine. That melted me. Family was something that I saw I was going to have to get used to. It was new to me. I had grown up inside of a broken home from the day I was born. All I knew was dysfunction. But I was sure I would get to where I needed to be for my immediate family.

Bubbie rubbed my abs. "So, baby, what are you going to get into today?"

"I don't know. I thank I'ma roll around the city and see what it is. I wanna holler at Phoenix and see what he got for me. I've been gone for five, so it better be a nice amount." I pulled Jahmya down and held her in my right arm like a football. My lips pressed to her forehead every few minutes. She was so precious to me.

"Phoenix? Aw shit, here we go, man. So what you thanking you finna do, get back in those streets? Ain't you supposed to be working on finishing up that *Cutthroat Mafia* series?"

I nodded. "Yeah, I got parts one and two done. All I gotta do is put the finishing touches on part three. In order to do that, I'ma have to fly out to Baltimore and spend some time with my cousin Payton. Them niggas really in the field, and he gon' give me the full run down. After that, sometime next month I gotta fly out to the A and see how Ca$h wanna do this movie shit. But before I do any of that, I gotta get everythang situated here. What our funds looking like?"

Bubbie broke eye contact with me and sat up in the bed before climbing off of it. "We doing good."

I kissed Jahmya's forehead again before laying her on the side of the bed beside me. "What that mean?" Since I was in prison, I'd decided to allow Bubbie to control and handle our finances. As long as she kept me with a few G's on my books every month, I didn't care what else she did with the money, as long as all of our bills were paid and my kids stayed fresh. I knew that I was pulling in no less than ten to fifteen thousand from Lock Down Publications every month, and that was the bare minimum. Every three months when the paperback side of money came in, it was pushed up to no less than twenty to twenty five G's. This had been consistent for every bit of two years, so we should have been good. I knew that for sure, but the way she was acting had me feeling a way.

"Dang, boy, you just love arguing, don't you?" She rolled her eyes and got ready to walk out of the room.

I jumped up and caught her before she hit the door. I took a hold of her wrist. "Stop playing wit' me, Bubbie. What's good wit' my bread?"

She jerked her wrist away and mugged me. "Aw, so now, it's just your money, really?"

I looked back to the bed where our daughter was, and I wanted to make sure that she was still asleep before I wilded the fuck out. She was. I turned back to Bubbie and got ready to jack her little ass up. "Shawty, if you keep playing with me, I swear to God, I'm about to do some shit that's gon' shatter us. Now what's good with my money?"

"JaMichael, my mama got into some trouble. They were trying to take her mansion, her cars, and a bunch of her assets for tax evasion. She was facing seven years in prison."

"What the fuck that got to do with me?" I hemmed her ass against the wall. "What the fuck is you saying?"

"She gon' pay us back. Her restaurant just taking a dive right now because of this whole pandemic thing. But after they find a vaccine, everything is going to go back to normal, and she is going to pay us back what she owes up and the five percent interest."

I released her. "How much did you give her? Naw, scratch that, what do we have in the bank right now?"

"We got fifty-five thousand left."

"Fifty-five thousand! That's it? With all those ma'fuckin' books I got? How much did you give this bitch?" I snapped and woke up Jahmya. She woke up crying and looking around for me, I imagine.

"JaMichael! That is my mother. Watch what you call her."

I picked Jahmya up and bounced her up and down in my arms. "Man, shawty, the last thing you need to be doing right now is telling me what I need to be doing. How much did you give her of my money?"

"Two hundred thousand. And I thought it was our money. I don't even know why you're tripping. You make damn near twenty or thirty thousand dollars every month. That chump change'll come back to us in no time."

"Bubbie, listen to me. Get out of my face. It seems like I am steadily finding out more and more bullshit every single day, and it ain't even been twenty-four hours yet. We only got fifty-five G's to our name. That ain't no money. Not wit' three kids and two high maintenance-ass parents." I covered

Jahmya's ears when I said the last part that involved swear words.

Bubbie placed her hand on her hip. "JaMichael, it's a pandemic. Most families wish they could have what we have put up, and it's like I said, my mother is going to pay us back so we don't have anything to worry about. Damn, stop tripping." The doorbell rang, and she left out of the bedroom.

I sat on the edge of the bed, fuming. I held Jahmya in my arms. Had I not been holding my li'l princess, I was sure that I would have gone off on the deep end real fast. I felt like Bubbie was keeping more than a few secrets, and that was starting to make me look at her different. How the fuck could you lend two hundred thousand dollars out of somebody else's money? That shit didn't make sense to me.

I picked up Jahmya and we headed downstairs to see who the hell was ringing the doorbell that early in the morning. When I got to the bottom step right behind the open door, I could hear Bubbie talking to somebody. My ears perked up.

"Nawl, see, you don't listen. I told you that he was getting out yesterday, not Friday. You need to open up those big-ass ears." She laughed.

"Aw, now since he's home, my ears big? Really, that's how we finna play dis shit?" a male voice returned.

"I'm just playing wit' you. Don't start getting all sensitive on me now. Ain't nothing changed," Bubbie said and then paused for a minute. "So are you ready to meet him?"

"Yeah, I ain't worried about shit. Just don't switch up on me, and we good. You already know I got the purest intentions. Come here." He laughed and it sounded like he pulled her to him.

When I stepped in front of the door, they were hugging - Bubbie and some light caramel nigga with sandy brown dreadlocks and tattoos all over his neck and arms. He held her close and kissed her cheek, whispering in her ear. She laughed and popped his shoulder. I stood there getting madder and madder. Then he looked up and saw me before backing up.

Chapter 6

Bubbie looked back and saw me staring at her with Jahmya in my arms. Her eyes got big. She looked back over to him, and then to me again. She swallowed her spit. "Uh, hey baby, this is your cousin, Kool Aid."

Kool Aid nodded his head in an upward motion. He came to the doorway and extended his hand. "What up, li'l cuz? I heard a gang about you. It's about time I can connect the man to the legacy."

"I'ma let y'all talk for a minute. Come on, baby." Bubbie came and took Jahmya out of my arms. She slipped past me and disappeared into the house.

I took one look at her over my shoulder, and a deep feeling of disdain and anger came over me. But at the same time, there was a sense of calm and peace. There was no doubt in my mind that there was something very familiar about the two of them. The way he was holding her wasn't like a family member. Nawl, he was holding her as if they had fucked around on more than a few occasions.

"Say cuz, do you mind if we roll for a minute?" Kool Aid asked, looking me over with a slight smirk on his face.

I nodded. "Yeah, gimme a minute to get dressed and I'll be right down."

***

After a half hour, I came down the steps and walked up to his black Benz truck. I slipped inside, and his loud music got to pounding at my head almost immediately. He was banging the new NBA Youngboy album. The seatbelt came across my chest and he pulled off, turning the music down at the same time. I was thankful for that 'cause I really wasn't feeling that shit he was bumping. I was a Memphis nigga - Yo Gotti and Moneybagg crazy.

"Damn, so you're my uncle Taurus's son? His only one, at that. Damn."

"Yep, as far as I know. And are you Juice's?" I didn't know much about my uncle Juice like that, other than the fact that he was supposed to have been a straight Savage, and he and my father Taurus were rivals. Even thinking about that fact had me wondering why the fuck Kool Aid would be trying to get so close to my family.

"Yeah, I guess I am. I mean, I don't really know because they say my pops was out here in these streets fa' real, mane. But since I been alive, ain't no other nigga came up to me and told me that he was my brother, so…" He shrugged his shoulders.

"That's what's up. What about sisters?" I asked, even though I really didn't give a fuck. I was just trying to buy time until my temper calmed down a little bit. I kept imagining the two of them on the porch, and it was causing me to become heated.

"Yeah, I got two sisters, and both are from my pops. Sia and Saleyah. They're twins. They just turned eighteen three days ago. They recently moved to Memphis from New Orleans with their mother. I already know they gon' wanna meet you."

"Oh yeah? Why is that?" I asked dryly, looking around the streets as we drove past them.

"Because all the family talk about is Taurus. Everybody wanna know what his seed looks and acts like. Except me, that is. I'm my own man. I don't get caught up in all of that shit. I'm tryna build my own legacy." He kept rolling.

"I hear that." Everywhere I looked, I could see that the city of Memphis was in ruins. Stores were boarded up, along with houses. Restaurants had windows that were broken out. A bunch of houses and businesses had been set on fire, and there seemed to be so many people walking around with dirty clothes and shoes. They appeared to be broke and homeless. The city had a dead ambiance that made my stomach turn over. This wasn't the Memphis that I was familiar with. "What happened to the city?"

"That's that Coronavirus, man. Ever since that shit hit, the city been dying. It seems like everybody shooting heroin now, or doing meth. There are so many sick and broke people that it ain't funny. It sucks." He looked around at the sights that I was looking over. "There is only so much money out here now, and the little bit that it is, a ma'fucka'll kill you for it." He laughed and shook his head. "Speaking of which, what are you trying to do now that you're home?"

I was lost in the make-up of the city. My heart was heavy for my homeland. "What do you mean?"

"Word is that before you left is that you had a bunch of niggas rolling under you that called themselves the Heartless Goons. I heard y'all was getting major money out there in Orange Mound. Phoenix run dat bitch right now, but he fuck with me the long way, so it's good. On top of that, we're all family, so it shouldn't be nothing for us to get money and bring some sort of esteem to the Stevens name. I mean, I'm wit' it."

Ever since I was a young nigga, Orange Mound had been a part of my heart. I was born there and raised in the heart of it. Although Phoenix was my cousin, I didn't care about that when it came to supremacy. I was all about me and my pockets. A broke nigga in the south didn't get no respect, and I wasn't with that broke shit.

"So I think the best bet for you, now that you're home, and I can imagine probably fucked up a li'l bit, is to link up with Phoenix and his Duffel Bag Cartel. Them niggas raking in hundreds of thousands of dollars at a time. In a few months, you should be sitting lovely."

Whenever a nigga said that he was fucked up, that meant that he was broke and down on his luck. I may have just gotten out of the joint, but I didn't feel like I was fucked up. "Dawg, what make you thank I'm fucked up?"

"You just got out. I know Bubbie ain't seeing no cash like that because she gotta provide for those babies all the time, so she ain't working. Where else yo' dough gon' come from?" He looked over at me with an eyebrow raised.

"Nigga, I got books. I ain't just in the streets. I got books all over the world." I had to buss his head to let him know that I wasn't a regular nigga like him that needed the streets in order to survive. While I was a street nigga, I still knew how to expand my hustle.

"Books, yeah, she told me about them. Say, you bag about fifteen to thirty bands a month. That's awright, but it's still chump change." He laughed. "Nigga, you got three kids, and yo' baby mother about the finer thangs in life. Fifteen to thirty ain't no money. And you know it ain't." He broke up laughing.

I got heated real fast. "Nigga, why you know so much about my ma'fuckin' bidness? What, shawty just sat around telling you everythang 'bout me 'cause y'all ain't have shit else to talk about?"

Kool Aid swerved through traffic and pulled up on the side of three females sitting inside of a pink drop top Benz sitting on thirty-two inch gold Forgiatos. He turned up his music and beeped the horn at them. The driver looked up and smiled, then she went back to looking out at the road, seeming to ignore him. The passenger threw her arms up, and the female in the back seat busted up laughing. All of them were redbones and fine as fuck from as far as I could see. Kool Aid beeped his born again and told them to pull over. The passenger whispered to the driver, and finally the driver pointed to the side street ahead. They pulled over, and Kool Aid pulled in back of them.

He placed his black Coronavirus mask over his face and reached under his seat, pulling up a chrome .45. He cocked it. "Say, li'l cuz, when I get out, just pull off in my shit and meet me at the lake down the street from Orange Mound in fifteen minutes. You ain't got shit to do with this. I told this nigga I was gon' catch his people slipping one by one. My word is everything." He got out of the car.

Before I could say anything, he had already jumped out of the truck. He walked casually along the side of it. The females were flirting and saying all kinds of things to him. I couldn't tell if he was responding or not. The next thing I knew, he upped his gun. The females froze. They threw their hands up in the air. Kool Aid started waving his gun wildly. Two of the females hopped out of the car and broke off running. Kool Aid pulled the driver out of the car. He stood her straight up, placed the gun under her chin, and pulled the trigger. The top of her head exploded. She slumped to the ground in a puddle of blood.

I drove off. I looked back into the rearview mirror as he began to chase the other two females, bussing at them. "What the fuck wrong wit' dis nigga?" I glanced back into the rearview mirror again. He'd caught the female that had been in the back seat and gunned her down. She lay in the middle of the street twitching. He took off behind the other one. I turned the corner and got back on the busy street of Martin Luther King Drive with my heart racing.

***

Kool Aid pulled up alongside me thirty minutes later in a new change of clothes and a new Benz. He hopped out of it, and two Mexicans hopped out with him. He knocked on the driver's window. He looked both ways with a serious look upon his face.

I rolled it down. "What's good, Blood?"

"Say, we gotta jump in dis shit right here. Bruh n'em finna take that bitch and buss it down."

I gathered my things and jumped out of it. I walked up to that nigga. "Dawg, you cool?"

He laughed and got into the driver's seat of the black Benz and unlocked my door for me. "Yeah, I'm good. We gotta roll over to Orange Mound. Phoenix saying he wanna touch bases wit' you before we turn in. Then I wanna introduce you to my fam so they can quit bugging me. You ready to roll?" He asked this as I got in and clicked my seatbelt in place.

"Nigga, you ain't finna say shit 'bout them bitches that you just fanned down?"

He backed the Benz out of the parking spot as the Mexicans drove away with his truck. He pulled out of the Lake Fronts parking lot and sped down the street, coming to a halt at the lights. "Mane, what's known need not be explained. But I'll break down the move for you since you're my cousin. I get that paper to slump shit."

"What?"

"Yeah, ever since I came up here from Louisiana, I been fucking wit' the Duffel Bag Cartel on that slumping shit. It's me and a few of my Nawlins potnas that run under me. We call ourselves the Slump Gods. Whenever Phoenix need some shit handled, and I don't give a fuck whether it's a nigga, bitch, or a kid, I make that shit happen. Every job got a certain pay to it. I get more for women and twice as much for shawties. Depending on how high the nigga is, I can get as much as thirty G's for a hit. Sometimes, Phoenix'll have me slump four people in a week. He ain't risking nobody fucking with his Cartel or the money flow, and I can't blame him because it's hard out here. So as long as he keep that money coming right, my guns'll keep doing the job for the homie. It's as simple as that." He pulled on to the strip of Orange Mound. "Those bitches I hit back there were going to testify at court against a few members of the crew. I been trying to get up with them for forty-eight hours already. That's all he gives me to do a job is that. If I don't finish it in forty-eight hours, he hires somebody else, and I lose money. Not only that, but he starts to look at me differently. That could mean death. So I never go forty-eight hours without getting the job done." He smiled as he was saying this last part. "Yeah, but that's enough about me. He wanna holler at you, I'm sure to see what you're trying to do out here. Y'all need to get an understanding quick because once these other turn coat-ass niggas see that you're home, they gonna wanna jump on yo' ship. Phoenix be handling ma'fuckas real rough, and every day it feels like he be ready to take his own workers out of the game. So choose yo' side, my nigga, that's all I can tell you. But don't act like you're posing a threat to his money. That's a no-no. That threat'll get you fucked up and over. Words from the wise."

I side-eyed that nigga and nodded. I didn't give a fuck what type of shit Phoenix had going on now. I was still me, and I didn't bow down to no man or no bitch. That nigga Phoenix didn't spook me in no way. I would play my role accordingly until I saw my in, and when I did, I was coming back for my slot. That was the real. Fuck everything else.

Ghost

Chapter 7

Phoenix was caramel-skinned with almond-slanted eyes and short curly hair that was shaved into a style on the sides. He was fit, muscle bound, and he had tattoos all over him, just like most of the niggas in Memphis. He was sitting at the head of a long wooden table with a blunt in his mouth and a pile of money in front of him, and two armed bodyguards stood behind him. Kool Aid and I walked into his one of many trap houses throughout Memphis.

"Say mane, I know that ain't my li'l cousin JaMichael right thurr?" He set the blunt in the ashtray and stood up with a big smile on his face.

His teeth were covered in white gold, and he had diamonds on each tooth. I didn't know if they were permanent or snatch outs, but his grill was sparkling as if he'd just gotten them done. I could tell that he was doing quite well for himself since I'd left the scene five years ago.

"Yeah, it's me." I smiled, playing my role. "And I hope you happy to see a nigga 'cause I'm fucked up." There that expression was again that I hated, but found necessary to use within this manipulative situation.

Phoenix came around the table and hugged me. He held me longer than normal. "Damn, nigga, what was you doing, lifting every weight you could find in that ma'fucka'?" He laughed.

I shook my head. "Nawl, but when you locked in the bing, that's all you can do is lift weights and find ways to strengthen your mind. If you don't, you'll wind up taking medication or going crazy. I saw a lot of niggas fold when it came time for that cell to close for the night."

Phoenix lowered his head. "Damn, that's fucked up. That's why I'm holding court in the streets. I'ma make Twelve kill me. I can't see myself pulling even another month in prison. I did about five, and that shit took a chunk out of my soul. It's amazing to see you standing before me as strong as you are. That's what's good, playboy." He rested his hand on my shoulder. "I see you done set the hood book world on fire!"

I cringed. I hated when people called my books "hood books". To me it felt like because these books were written in truth, about our people, and where we come from, that people often found a way to demoralize them or to make them seem as if they are nothing more than ghetto filth, all because they came from the mind of people of color. You had ma'fuckas like Stephen King writing about killing whole families, monsters, and all types of weird shit, and his books were classified as regular fiction whereas mine were considered "urban or hood fiction" all because of the pigment of my skin, but that's another story.

Phoenix nodded his head. "Every time something drop, I make sure every nigga in Memphis go get that shit. When it came to your Duffel Bag Cartel series, at first I thought you were exposing too much of our bidness, but then one of my lawyers told me that as long as you leave it under the guise of fiction that we will be cool. That's why I sent you those letters asking you to dumb it down a little bit. You remember?"

I nodded. "Yeah, I do, and I did, for the most part. Anyway, what you got for me?" I didn't feel like doing no weak-ass song and dance with him. I didn't really like Phoenix. In my opinion, I still felt like he had something to do with Jahliyah getting kidnapped by Mikey, and I've felt since day one that Phoenix is just phony. I ain't never been one to blow smoke up another nigga's ass, so I had to get to the money quick. That was all I really cared about.

"Damn, look at you. You come right out with it, don't you?" Phoenix looked around the room at all those that were present.

"Ain't no reason for me not to, You sitting over there with a table full of money. I'm just touching down, and I gotta get right. Shit ain't what it should be at the crib."

Phoenix mugged Kool Aid. "Say, Blood, I thought you was making sure that Bubbie and his seeds were straight?"

Kool Aid grew defensive. "I was. I made sure that whenever you sent me out with bread for their bills that she got that shit. I don't know what he's talking about."

I side-eyed Kool Aid. "Phoenix, how often was you paying my shawty bills?"

"Every month. I made sure that I sent li'l homie over thurr wit' three G's each month to give to her. I done already touched bases wit'; the landlord over there. The mortgage ain't nothing but a gee a month. That leaves two for the rest of the bills. Then I already know you eating from Lock Down Publications, so I didn't really thank to send no dough yo' way while you were in there. I knew you were good, but I did ask, through Kool Aid, and he told me that Bubbie said she had you, and that you were beyond straight. Was she lying?"

I shook my head. "Nawl, I was good."

"Then why are you making that ugly-ass face?" Phoenix laughed and took a seat back in his chair. He ushered for us to sit down.

I sat and pulled up my seat to the table. There was a pile of hundred dollar bills in front of me. By eye, I counted no less than twenty G's with the quickness. And that was just the money that was in front of me. There were hundreds spread out all along the table. "Nawl, shit just a li'l funny to me, that's all."

"Yeah, I can feel that. But let me ask you something, cuz, what do you need?" Phoenix picked up his blunt and took three strong pulls off of it.

"I need some real bread. I got a li'l bit of nothing put up, but it ain't shit that I'm used to. You already know that I'm a man that's used to leading an army of money getters." I looked across the table at Kool Aid and then down to Phoenix.

Phoenix sucked his teeth. "Ain't we all?" He blew the weed smoke out of his nostrils and sat back. "Nigga, you're used to running Orange Mound, but that shit ain't happening no more." He frowned and leaned forward in his chair. "You see, the way that this Coronavirus shit is operating, it's putting plenty niggas out of work, and out of business. If a ma'fucka ain't recession proof, then they are in for a rude awakening." He looked over the table. "As you can see, I don't know what the fuck a recession is. I been getting money in the heartland. Shid, as a matter fact of fact, I been getting money in this heart land, and I've been all in other nigga's shit too catching back ends in their shit. If it even looks like a ma'fucka these days pose a threat to me, that's what I got hittas for. Ain't that right, li'l cuz?"

"You muthafuckin' right," Kool Aid returned.

"You see, back in the day, JaMichael, I didn't have the game all figured out like I do now. I didn't know how to play this bitch like a fiddle, but I got this now, and ain't no ma'fucka gon' take shit from me or this Duffel Bag Cartel. Bitch nigga wanna try dat and they can get it in blood. Real talk." He mugged his hittas that were standing behind him before he turned back to me. "When it comes to you, I ain't forget our past, but I'm trying my best to let it go so that we can look forward to a productive future. I mean, after all, we are family, and if I'm eating, then we all should be eating, and I ain't talking about no thirty G's a month book money. I'm

62

talking a hundred G's or better." He curled the right side of his upper lip. "Guess my question to you is, what are you trying to do? Are you trying to jump on board with this Duffel Bag shit, or are you still on that Heartless Goon nonsense that you were on before you left the bricks five years ago?"

Now a cocky, hot-headed stupid nigga, would have acted all tough and repped his gang to the fullest just to be gunned down in a matter of days, and if he wasn't gunned down, there surely was no way for him to be able to slip into the cusp of all of the money that Phoenix and his crew was accruing without exposing his hand. Me, I was no dumb nigga. I knew that I couldn't get back to where I wanted to be without having major money, and that broke shit wasn't in me at all.

"Bruh, I come to you with palms up. We're family. I'm trying to eat. I denounce all that other shit that wasn't feeding me or my family when I was on lock. I know what our past was, and that shit was just some young shit. You showed me who you really was by making sure that my people were straight when I was in there. Didn't any nigga from the Heartless Goons do that."

"It's probably 'cause they were heartless." Kool Aid said this and busted up laughing.

Phoenix thought about it for a minute, and then he joined into the laughter as well. I saw myself killing the both of them. I didn't like or care about either one of these niggas. I didn't care if they were my family or not. I sat there with my tail tucked for two minutes while they laughed and laughed like they'd lost their freaking minds.

Phoenix was the first to go serious. "I'ma put you up in Black Haven."

"Black Haven? I don't know shit about Black Haven. I'm an Orange Mound nigga, have been my whole life," I said, already imagining how fucked-up and run down Black Haven was. I was taught to hate niggas from that hood, even though I never allowed myself to because I have always been about the money and never about disliking another nigga just because of where he was from. I felt dudes that got all into that gangbanging shit never really got the chance to see the right amount of money that they could if they simply just left that banging shit out of the equation.

"I know where you're from, and I know what you're used to. That's why I don't want you nowhere near Orange Mound. I'm selfish with that turf now. I don't want nobody operating in or out of my shit other than me. I know it's gon' make you feel a way, but you'll get over it." He sat back. "If you ain't feeling that you could always stay fucked up."

I smiled. "Yeah, that is an option, huh?"

"Sho' is. So what are you going to do?" Phoenix crossed his fingers and looked down the table at me.

"I'ma take that spot and rock that bitch. I ain't got no other choice. I appreciate you, dawg." I got up, and he stood as well. We embraced, "I'm serious. I appreciate you, bruh."

"Yeah, I know, and it's all good. Just don't bite the hand that feeds you. There is a whole new system in place now. So that won't be in your best interest." He released me. "I'ma give you a week to assemble your own crew, and then I'ma show you where we gon' let you do your thing under the Duffel Bag Cartel, is that clear?"

I nodded. "Crystal."

"Awright. Until den, take this credit card and get your clothing game up to par. I can't have my blood out here looking popped and shit. That makes me look bad." He handed me a Capitol One card with the information to it already taped on the back. Then he dismissed me from his trap like I was a regular bum type nigga.

I left feeling vengeful and in a way. I had to get back to where I had fallen from. There was no other way around it.

***

I stayed up late that night, long after Bubbie had already fallen asleep, and my mind wandered all over the place. I hated that I had found myself right back on the same path that I had been on before I'd gotten locked up, but I just couldn't imagine myself being swallowed up by the new normal that was America, where the average person was broke and down on their luck.

Even though I had a few chips in the bank, every time I factored in how much it cost to provide for a family of four, and how hard it was going to be to provide for them by legal means, I just couldn't see it. I knew for a fact that I didn't have that regular or settling shit inside of me. I liked to live well. I loved designer and making sure that my family had top of the line everything. I didn't wanna see Bubbie shopping at discount stores for their shoes and clothes. Not that anything was wrong with the people that did, but I just didn't want my people shopping there, or settling for such a life. I felt that as a man that would make me less than.

So my only option, besides my books, was to hit up the slums of Memphis and to conquer it by any and every means. If Phoenix was willing to give me Black Haven, then I would take it, and make it the new Orange Mound, before I came for the actual Orange Mound that he swore up and down he ran with an iron fist. Yeah, it was the only way. As long as I allowed him to see me as a person depending on him, he would fail to see me as a threat, so I'd play into his ignorance. I'd reign the submissive and appreciative role until I felt it was my moment to take over the game and to crush him like I should have done before I got knocked and went down for five years. Damn, I hated feeling inferior to any man, especially one I'd already made bow down.

I laid there feeling so vindictive and so murderous that I had to get out of the bed. I was starting to shake, and I didn't want to wake Bubbie, so I climbed out of the bed and I went into Jahmya's room. I found her lying on her side, breathing lightly. I sat on her bed and I picked her up ever so slightly, then I laid back down and I placed her on my chest.

She jerked and opened her eyes for a second. When she saw that it was me, she closed her eyes back and smiled. "I love you, Daddy."

That made my heart melt. "I love you too, Princess. You are my whole world." I kissed her four-year-old forehead and closed my eyes with my arms wrapped around my baby. I became calm, and serene. The killa that was threatening to break free slowly started to dissipate. I stopped shaking, and after what seemed like a million years, I fell asleep and drifted off with my arms protectively around her.

Chapter 8

Two weeks later, I'd taken twenty young hustlers from Orange Mound that I vetted over to Black Haven with me and we opened up shop. Phoenix already had a stranglehold on the projects anyway, and before he put me in place, he made sure that everybody knew that I was his cousin and that Taurus was my pops, and that he was allowing for me to run Black Haven, while he took the full reins in Orange Mound. I got a few dirty looks from a few of the dope boys that I could tell had been there their entire lives, but that was about it.

On the second day of the first week, Phoenix had a shipment of twenty kilos of some of the strongest Sinaloa Tar heroin dropped off to me. The product was ninety percent, and I acted as if I had never left. I sat in the trap with my dope boys, and we bussed those bricks down in record time. We stepped on them once to double the profits, and left the potency level at about seventy-five percent, which was still good, I knew for sure that the addicts wouldn't trip, especially because there was a drought going on all over Memphis, and the only people that were able to produce anything was the Duffel Bag Cartel.

We took the work and bagged it all up into dime bags that were usually sold for ten dollars, but we sold them for seven. When the word got out of how we were rocking, the projects went crazy, and we wound up having lines all around the block in a matter of five days. I sat back and watched the operations for a full week, before I was sure that my li'l homies could handle themselves. Then I went on to the next trap and ran the same gambit. By the end of the second week, I had eight traps jumping and a few dope boys riding around in cars making deliveries with Coronavirus masks on their faces.

By the end of the first month, I had fifteen traps jumping and twenty dope boys rolling all around Memphis making deliveries. The money started to come in fast as it had before, and I found myself right back in the swing of things. It felt good to be counting cold hard cash again. It felt good to be stuffing book bags of money and taking them to the crib for Bubbie to count. As much as I hated myself for being in love with the trap, I couldn't help it. That shit was in my soul.

***

It was a sunny day with the barely any clouds in the sky, and on this particular day, I was walking around the Mercedes Benz dealership looking for a nice truck I could jump into when out of nowhere, Saleyah came out of the building and into the parking lot dressed in her business skirt dress with a Gucci Coronavirus mask across her face. I was sizing this black-on-black Benz truck up and down, ready to move in on the buy, when something told me to turn around.

"Dang, you ain't been out for more than two months, and already you're about to cop a 2021 Benz, big boy? Look at you." She smiled with her hair slightly blowing in the wind.

I turned all the way around and walked toward her. "Damn, what's good with you, cuz? What are you doing here?"

She walked closer and stopped. "I thought you knew that I worked here. What, Kool Aid didn't tell you?"

I shook my head. "What would he be telling me your business for? We don't even talk about shit but the trap. Where my hug at?" I held my arms open.

She walked into them and wrapped her arms around my neck. "Hey cuz."

I held her frame for a moment, and damn, she felt good. Saleyah reminded me of a prettier version of Doja Cat. They had the same figure, but Saleyah was more fit. "Damn, I bet you be giving these li'l niggas all they can handle, don't you?"

She laughed. "You already know that my mother and my brother don't let me go anywhere. I wish they did, but they don't. I'm a lame homebody. It is what it is though. What are you looking for?" She slid out of my embrace and walked over to the truck.

On accident, my eyes trailed down to the way her skirt was fitting her frame. Her ass looked like it was trying to buss out of it. "Damn."

She looked over her shoulder at me. "What?"

"Nawl, I was just admiring the whip, that's all. Anyway, what you thank 'bout dis boy right here? You thank I'd kill the game with this ma'fucka?"

She nodded. "Yeah, we just rolled this one out here yesterday, fresh off the showroom floor. This will shut the city down. All you gotta do is put your music in it and get your ground effects game up to par. I'm thinking that since the truck is black-on-black that you should get a purple light to go underneath it."

"Hell yeah, that sounds about right. But I'm saying, since you work here and everythang, you thank you can get them to come down off of the sticker price?" I asked, following behind her and not taking my eyes off of that ass. I knew I was bogus because she was Kool Aid's baby sister, but I didn't care. She was thick as a ma'fucka, and all I was doing was simply looking.

"I think I can do that for you. But if I do this for you, you gotta help me out too." She turned around and walked up to me. Her perfume got louder.

"What's good? Anything you need. I promise."

She looked into my eyes with her light brown ones. "Are you sure?"

"Yeah, as long as you get them to come down about five to ten G's, I got whatever you need." I didn't know exactly what she was going to need, but whatever it was, I was gon' try my best to make it happen.

"That's easy. I get an employee discount, and because you're my cousin you can get twenty-five percent off of the sticker price. That's more than eleven thousand."

My eyes lit up. I didn't wanna hear Bubbie's mouth about me buying a new whip without asking her and her feeling like I had spent too much too soon. But now that I was getting a whole-ass eleven bands off of the sticker price, I didn't give a fuck what she was going to say. "That's a bet, cuz. Now what can I do for you?"

She bit on her fingernail. Her eyes burned a hole into mine, and then she looked off. "I'm scared to ask you."

"Scared? Girl, for what. You can ask me anything." I slipped behind her and wrapped my arm around her neck. "Talk to me, shawty."

"Okay, well, you already know how strict my mother is. And because I'm going to college online and still living under her roof, she feels like she can tell me what to do all of the time, and she kind of can, but I digress." She paused again.

"Gon' 'head and spit it out."

"Okay, cuz, I need you to get her off of my back, and if you can't do that, I need for you to help me get some space so that I can spend some time with my girlfriend."

"Girlfriend?"

She nodded her head. "Yeah, girlfriend, what's the matter with that?"

"You mean like a female that's your friend, or your actual girlfriend?"

"I mean a female that I am dating, or at least trying to date, but my mother is making it really hard. Why are you freaking out? I have no preference."

"I ain't freaking out, I was just caught off guard, but say no more. I got you. Just hit me up when you're trying to spend some time with her, and I'll make sure that you get the chance to."

She squealed and hugged my neck. "Thank you, big cuz. Oh, and I'm not supposed to tell you this because it's extremely creepy to me, but my mother has an insane crush on you." She stuck her finger down her throat and gagged. "All she talks about is Taurus, and how fine he was, and how you look just like him. She talked about you so much the first night that we all met you for the first time that Kool Aid told her to shut up. Then she slapped him and made him leave, but yeah. She's weak over you. You know, just for your information. Now let's get inside and do this paperwork. I'ma make sure that you get everything you want out of this deal and more." She winked and grabbed ahold of my hand, pulling me along to the office. Once again my eyes trailed down to her fat-ass booty that had that skirt jiggling in the back like crazy.

***

"So let me get this straight. You done took yo' crazy ass out of this house and copped a sixty thousand dollar whip without telling me? Then you took it upon yourself to spend fifty more thousand dollars for the rims and twenty more for the sounds inside of it, and you didn't think that none of this was worth discussing with me before you did it?"

"Nawl, this is my gift to myself. I knocked down five long years in the bing. I came out alive, and strong. The least

I could do was cop me something fresh off the lot. This ma'fucka say, nigga, you on somethin'."

Bubbie came out into the middle of the street where I was standing, admiring my truck that I had to take into the shop first thing in the morning, so it could get the total package. She was shaking her head. "JaMichael, we have three kids right there in that house. You can't afford this, and you ain't keeping it. Take it back."

"You got me fucked up. I don't care how many kids I got. I can afford this. I just brought yo' ass two duffel bags full of cash that you ain't even counted yet. Plus, I got plans on stacking up my safes before the month is out. I ain't no petty hustler. I got this. You just fall in line."

"Fall in line? No the fuck he didn't just say fall in line." She turned around in a circle as if she was losing her mind. "Nigga, I been standing in line for the last five years for your ass. I stood in lines when it came time to visit you. I stood in lines when it came time to put money on your books. I stood in line when it came time to sell your books out the trunk of my fuckin' car when things weren't going so well in the beginning and I was going through all kinds of financial crisis that I didn't let you know anything about, because I didn't want your bid to be harder than it already had to be.

But now that you're home, living under the same roof with me, you got the nerve to say what you just said to somebody who's been holding your crazy ass down since day one. No the fuck you didn't." She turned all the way around in a circle again, leaned down, and smacked the pavement. Then she stood up and started to walk around the truck. "Aw yeah, I see what this ma'fucka is right here. This must be for me. This must be for me standing by you like a trooper. Am I right?"

I had my right hand over my forehead. Shawty was driving me absolutely crazy, and I think she knew that she was too because she had a slight smirk on her face that was irritating me. "Say, Bubbie, get off of that bullshit. I don't feel like going through all of this unnecessary bullshit with you. I copped me a whip I can get around in. I been bussing my ass ever since I touched down without ceasing. Had you not given your mother my money to begin with, I would have been able to come out of prison with a brand new whip waiting on me, but since you chose her over us, this is what I had to do. So fall yo' li'l ass back, shawty, 'cause this shit is happening." I mugged her and turned my eyes back to my truck.

Bubbie stood there for a moment with her head lowered. She got to mumbling to herself, and then she balled her fists and started to punch her hand. "This muthafucka bout to make me catch a case. Lord, why you wanna lock me up and throw away the key? I know you died on the cross for me, but why now, Lord? Why? Do. You. Wanna. Test. Me?" she asked, looking up at the sky.

"Quit all that dramatic-ass shit and take yo' ass in the house, before you the neighbors coming all out and looking at us like we're stupid or something."

Bubbie eyed me with hatred. She slowly walked up on me and stopped. She looked me up and down with her right eyebrow raised. "Ever since you've been home, I ain't been feeling like you been giving me my just due for holding yo' ass down. One minute, you're accusing me of somethin', the next you're telling me that I don't have a say in what goes on with you even though I pushed three kids out of my body for you and stood by you for more than five years when didn't nobody else wanted to. You treating me like I'm some punk bitch, JaMichael, and I don't like it. Nigga, you're forgetting that just like you're about that life, I am too. So if you're going to keep under-appreciating me, then I'ma do me, and I'ma let you do you. I worked too hard to be that bitch in your life, but if you ain't fuckin' wit' me, then fuck off. That's how I feel. You get what I'm saying?"

She had me boiling. "Over a truck? This how you're feeling 'cause I copped me a truck? That gold digging shit got you feeling like I'm shitting on you right now when I did everything to show you my gratitude."

She smacked her lips. "Your gratitude? How the fuck did you do that? I ain't seen no gratitude coming from yo' ass."

"What? Did you forget that from the day I stepped foot into the county jail that I was sending yo' ass G's to make sure that you kept some cash? I was paying all of our bills, even while I was locked in a cell. Whether it was directly or from somebody in my family that was doing it for me. Either way, you ain't had to pay shit since I been down."

She pointed her finger at my forehead. "Nigga, I got your three kids. That's yo' ma'fuckin' job to make sure I ain't gotta pay no bills. Fuck I look like paying bills when I gotta be a single mother while my man, the father to my children, is in prison? That doesn't make sense. Carrying yo' weight was the least you could do. Real talk."

"Real talk?" I laughed. "Shawty, ninety-nine percent of the niggas I was locked up had their bitch sending them money and taking out of their family's mouths. I'm the only one that was feeding mine. Real talk. And in the spirit of real talk, how many women know that their man in coming home and that he is already addicted the trap, a straight go-getter, would give two hundred thousand dollars of his money to her mother, or anybody else, just so he would have to come home a get right back into the game and pick up right where he left off? Explain that dumb-ass shit to me?"

She hung her head. "Here we go wit' this shit, again. Dwelling, man, ugh."

"Yeah, dwelling. Now you getting mad 'cause I copped me a whip. Typical. Well, I don't give a fuck. That boss shit is in my heart. This Benz truck is the latest to fuck over the Game, so I gotta be rolling it. You salty? You'll be awright. Tell yo' mother to send some of our cash back, and I'll cop you one, too. Until then, fall back." I opened the driver's door to my truck, ready to take it to get detailed.

She nodded. "Okay, JaMichael, I will. Nigga, do you. I'ma show you what it is though. You wanna open up this can of worms, you got it. Nigga, do you." She flipped both of her middle fingers in the air and headed upstairs and into our home.

As soon as she slammed the door, I felt like shit. I knew I should've handled it better, but my pride and my temper were a muthafucka.

Ghost

Chapter 9

Even though me and Bubbie stayed in the same house, we didn't say anything to each other for four days straight. When we came down the same hallway, she would turn sideways so I could get by, and I would do the same for her. During this time I felt so depressed, and yet so stubborn. I loved my baby, but I knew that if I caved in, it would open up the door for her to start standing on me, and I wasn't with that shit. I was tired of being in prison, and when it came down to a relationship, that was the one thing that scared me about them, the whole locked down factor. I mean, she was my life, and I'd smoke a nigga or bitch over her any day of the week, but I just couldn't see myself allowing for her to put those invisible shackles on me.

We didn't speak until the fifth day. That's when I came home at eleven at night and dropped a duffel bag full of cash in front of her while she was sitting on the couch braiding, Jahmya's hair. She looked up at me with those brown eyes, that to me said, "nigga, why the fuck are you bothering me?"

"Daddy, I don't wanna get my hair done. It hurts." For the first time I saw that my daughter had tears running down her cheeks. She looked like she was in a world of agony. "Can you help me, Daddy?"

I reached down to pick her up. Bubbie yanked harder on her hair and forced her to turn her head back straight. Jahmya started to cry heavy tears now. That shit made me feel so weak and wounded.

"Why you gotta be so rough with my baby?" I asked, crouching down in front of Jahmya and stroking her cheek.

"JaMichael, go on now. She ain't started crying until she heard your ass come through the door. And she can keep it up and I'ma pop her on those li'l legs," she threatened, looking down at our daughter that looked like a mini version of her. "And what am I supposed to do with this bag?"

"Aw, so since you salty at me, you ain't finna count the cash no more? Really, shawty?"

"Ain't none of it coming to me, so why should I even care what the total comes to?" She parted Jahmya's hair and greased that line of her scalp with coconut oil.

I sighed. Clearly she wanted to argue, and I ain't feel like going down that road with her. "Shawty, please, just count the money. You already know I don't trust nobody counting my cash other than you. Make it happen, and I'll be back in a minute to get the sum total." I kissed Jahmya on her cheek and stood up.

This seemed like it infuriated, Bubbie. She frowned and yanked Jahmya away from me slightly, then she went back to doing her hair. Jahmya was crying harder, yet silently so as to not get in more trouble, I imagined.

"I ain't counting that money, JaMichael. That ain't got nothin' to do with me no more. So when you come back, you're going to be faced with the same problem. It's in your best interest to get somebody else to do it. I'm not interested." She didn't even look up at me.

"Bubbie, can you please get off of that bullcrap. We are in this together. I need you."

"Now you need me." She rolled her eyes. "Well. I don't feel like being needed, and I don't want to be needed by you. Count yo' own damn money. Just make sure that when you're done that you pay these bills. As long as you do that, we ain't gotta say another word to each other." She waved me off. "Now go on."

I stood there for a moment, eyeing her closely. "Awright, well F you then. That's what you wanna be on." I grabbed the bag of money and headed out of the living room.

"Find you somebody else to fuck too, 'cause you ain't got that coming from me either. Do you, nigga, 'cause I'm definitely finna do me."

"Yeah, awright, just remember you said that shit. I'm out."

"Bye."

***

That night, I copped a money counter from Phoenix and I stayed up that night sending my bills through it. As long as I had the money to pay Phoenix back for the keys that he sold to me at wholesale prices, all of the other money was mine for the keeping. Of course I had a hell of an army to get right, and it took some mental financial maneuvering, but when it was all said and done, my take home after bussing that bag down was twenty G's to the good, which meant twenty G's for the safe. I was cool with that. Twenty G's in a week was nice take home cash.

***

Kool Aid hit me up at three o'clock in the morning the same night I finished counting all of that bread. He didn't even text me until he was right outside of my crib. Since I was still up, holding Jahmya while she slept, I decided to put her to bed and come down the stairs to meet him. When I jumped in the car he pulled right off and handed me a blunt.

"I hate to hit you up so early in the morning, JaMichael, but we got some bidness that we gotta take care of."

I put his blunt to my nose and sniffed the smoke to make sure that it was straight weed that I smelled. One thing about Memphis niggas was that they experimented with all kinds of drugs. It didn't matter what kind they were either. I wasn't tryna travel down that path. I didn't have any habits other than getting money, and I didn't want any either. So even though I smelled strictly bud coming out of his blunt, I hadn't seen him roll it, so I was good. "I'm straight, bruh. What brings you out here so late?"

"Phoenix wanted me to pull a job, and I need you to have my back. Plus, Phoenix thought that it would be a learning moment for you."

"A learning moment? Fuck he mean by that?"

Kool Aid shrugged his shoulders. "I don't know, cuz, I just relay the message. But anyway, he thought it was imperative that you tagged along to this hit. If you have a problem with the whole reason he wants you there, please take that shit up with him tomorrow or something. For now, let's buss this move."

I couldn't help frowning. "Where are we headed?"

"North Memphis. Phoenix had placed some nigga by the name of Scrappy in charge of his narcotics out there and apparently, Scrappy been dipping into the bags and stepping on his dope so much that word got back to Phoenix. Phoenix feels like Scrappy is ripping him off two different ways. One, by stepping on his dope so much that he is basically cutting everything in half and keeping the same amount of profit that Phoenix should be collecting from a potent product, and secondly by taking a few G's off the top of Phoenix's cash before every pick up. Phoenix also got word that this nigga done started his own Cartel of dope boys under himself. They ain't got shit to do with the Duffel Bag Cartel, and because of that, that means that the funds for our operation is going elsewhere. We can't have that, so I gotta ice this bitch nigga. That's what it is."

"And bruh thought that it was best that I was present to watch this whole thang?"

"Yep."

I nodded. "Cool, let's go." I felt like shots had been fired. The only reason I felt Phoenix wanted me to tag alone is so that he could send me a direct message, so in case I even thought about straying away from the original game plan that both he and I had already decided on, I would know that he wasn't going to play with me, and I would also have an image painted into my brain of what disloyalty would look like. I got his message loud and clear, and that shit only made me wanna get on some fuck shit earlier than I already had plans on doing. "How long until we're there?"

"Twenty minutes." Kool Aid looked me over.

I closed my eyes. "Cool, I'ma get some rest until then." The longer I kept my eyes open, the angrier I became, so I needed to close them or I was going to say some shit that I needed to keep to myself.

Ghost

Chapter 10

Kool Aid slipped the all-white ski mask over his face and handed me an identical one. He reached under his seat and pulled two .45s from it. He cocked both and placed them into holsters that were under his arms. Then he shocked the shit out of me when he pulled a tiny Ziploc bag of heroin out of his inside coat pocket. He dipped his pinky nail inside of it and tooted about a half a gram up each nostril. He tilted his head back and swallowed his spit. "I need that dog food, cuz. When I'm on this shit, I don't care about dropping nobody. Shawties, bitches, it is what it is. You wanna taste? It's ninety-five percent."

I mugged this dumb-ass nigga like he'd lost his mind. "Hell nawl, I don't fuck around, bruh. I gotta stay habit free. I got a whole-ass family to support."

"Nigga, I don't wanna hear all of that. A simple no is good enough for me." He tooted some more, rolled the Ziploc bag back up, and tucked it into his pocket. "Awright, you already see we finna have to creep in this bitch. I got the key. Just stay close by me. If anythang look funny, up and get to bussing. We'll sort out the problems, if there is any, at another time. Cool?"

"Yeah, cool. How much do you know this nigga that Phoenix got us ready to fan down?"

"I grew up seeing him in the hood. Ain't really no relation, but I have worked security for him on a few occasions. Fuck him though, let's roll."

We slipped out of the stolen Chevy Blazer and creeped down the dirty alley that was littered with all kinds of pissy couches, broken television sets, garbage, and dead cats that had lost their final battles with life. I stepped over as much bullshit as I could until we were in the backyard of Scrappy's trap. There was a fence that had a pit bull inside of it. The dog came running to the fence at full speed barking like it had lost its mind. I just knew the mission was dead. How in the fuck was we going to get into the yard, to be able to get into the house when there was a big-ass pit bull waiting to shake our asses?

Kool Aid played it cool. Instead of him panicking, he hopped the fence and jumped in front of the dog. The dog was so shocked that it stopped in its tracks. It looked over its shoulder, and then slowly backed up with its ears turned around. It lowered itself slightly to the ground and barked twice, then growled. Kool Aid didn't waste no time. He rushed the dog at full speed before the dog could jump up and run. Kool Aid scooped it up and wrapped his arm around its neck. He held it in the air and choked it out for two full minutes while its bottom legs kicked at him. Finally, he twisted the neck as hard as he could and snapped it. He flung the dog to the side of the yard and waved me to follow him.

I hopped the fence and glanced over at the dog twice before I hurried beside him. "Nigga, what the fuck is wrong with you? You ever seen that dog before?"

"Nope. But a dog is often the reflection of its owner. If the owner is a killa, then the dog would be also, but in this case, Scrappy ain't. So fuck it." He took out his keys and slid one into the lock real slowly.

I guess he felt his logic made sense. I didn't. The least I would have done was popped the pit and kept it moving, but to each his own.

As soon as the door opened, I slipped into the dark hallway behind Kool Aid. I pulled out my gun and cocked it after closing the door behind me. We went up the back steps that led into the first floor of the duplex. The door was locked.

Kool Aid slipped another key into this lock and slowly pushed it open as well. The door came open with a creak.

The first thing I smelled was the scent of primos. In Memphis, some of the locals had a habit of mixing their weed along with their coke. The two drugs had a way of counteracting off of each other and each drug caused the other one to last longer and to be stronger. The scent was so loud that I tried to hold my breath because that shit stank to me.

Kool Aid motioned for me to follow him again. He crouched down as we came through the kitchen and wound up in a little living room. The living room was empty. A television played with the sound off. We walked through the living room and I saw that there was a light on in the front room of the house. I could hear voices. A male and a female. The slight scent of alcohol came into the air, and the next thing I knew, we were running full speed into the front room and upping our guns on the pair inside of it.

"Freeze, muthafuckas! Don't either one of you move or make a sound!" Kool Aid snarled.

The female jumped up and screamed. "Oh my God!"

Boom.

Kool Aid sent a bullet right through her face. She fell over the table and curled into a ball. For some crazy reason she tried to cover the massive hole in her mug with both of her hands. But this didn't happen for long. She slowly straightened out her body before the life left her. Kool Aid stepped over her and aimed his smoking gun at Scrappy. "Say mane, you already know what time it is when that nigga Phoenix sends me. Fuck you got to say for yourself?"

Scrappy was about 5'6" tall. He was dark-skinned and chubby with a small afro and a big nose. He held his hands at shoulder length. "Say mane, I don't know why he would send you at me. I ain't did nothing wrong but be loyal to his ass. What is all of this about?"

The only thing that kept going through my mind is the fact that Kool Aid had left off a shot in the middle of the night. I was sure that somebody had to hear that. I got nervous. I still had five years of federal probation to do, and I didn't wanna get caught up with his crazy ass. I became antsy. "Say, handle that nigga and let's bounce, cuz. Straight up."

"I ain't did nothing, Kool Aid. Why would he send you at me?" Scrappy questioned.

"Bruh says you've been stepping on his dope way too much. He said that you're making the same amount of profits that he is when that ain't how that shit is supposed to go. Not only is you stretching his dope, but you're skimming off the top, and you got these niggas around north Memphis hollering Scrappy Gang. What the fuck is that about? You already know that this is Duffel Bag or nothing."

"That's a lie, homie. I ain't tryna start shit, and I don't know what he talking 'bout when it comes to skimming off the top or stretching his product. I do what he allows for me to do. And if a nigga hollering Scrappy Gang, that's 'cause I'm feeding they ass. That's their way of honoring me. That shit ain't got nothing to do with me. That's my word, bruh," Scrappy swore.

"Man, fuck that nigga. Smoke his bitch ass and let's keep it moving. Come on." I kept getting a bad feeling that something wasn't right.

"Don't kill me, Kool Aid. I been one hunnit to you. I ain't never told that nigga Phoenix about you and Alicia, and I never will. I ain't never told him how you been tearing off his traps. That shit doesn't concern me, but all I'm asking is that you let me skate on his one. Please. I'll make shit right with Phoenix. You got my word."

Kool Aid looked over his shoulder at me. He frowned and faced Scrappy. "Bitch nigga, that's how you put my bidness in the street?"

Something told me to look behind me, and boy am I glad that I did. When I turned around to look, my eyes got big, and then I was falling to the floor and aiming my gun at the two niggas that had slipped from the back room. One of them had a gauge in his hand and was seconds away from blowing my head off, since I was the closest, I imagined, before I dropped to the carpet and got to blowing his ass down.

Boom! Boom! Boom! Boom!

Fire spit from my gun, along with multiple bullets. They zipped from my gun and hit the gauge carrier all in the chest. He let off a big blast and then fell backward twitching on the carpet. His guy tried to break out of the kitchen and run. My slugs wet up his back and left him lifeless right in the kitchen's doorway.

"What the fuck?" Kool Aid had turned around to see what all of the commotion was about.

When he did, Scrappy took this as his cue to pull his .9 millimeter from under his shirt. He aimed and was a split second from pulling the trigger before my bullets knocked the left side of his face against the wall. Blood spurted across it, and his meat and flesh fell on the table. Kool Aid jumped back and shot up Scrappy's already lifeless body. The next thing I knew we were ransacking the house and minutes later, running out of it with two pillowcases full of money and dope.

***

Early the next morning, I was sleepy as fuck, and I could barely keep my eyes open. Phoenix stood over both me and

Kool Aid with a peculiar smile on his face. "That nigga thought shit was sweet, huh?"

I closed my eyes. If I could just get five minutes of sleep, I felt like I would have been good. "Yeah, I guess so, bruh."

"Yeah, but he doesn't anymore. I handled my bidness. I smoked the whole household. Ma'fuckas gon' know to not fuck wit' yo' paper, Phoenix, and I'd do that shit again with no hesitation. When you bite the hand that feed you, that's the least a nigga should get," Kool Aid jacked.

I opened my eyes and looked over at him. Was this fuck nigga really taking credit for my kills? That's what it seemed like. I wondered what angle he was really working. And what was Scrappy talking about when it came to Kool Aid supposedly ripping off Phoenix's traps?

"So you ain't have no problem handling dat bidness?" Phoenix asked with his right eyebrow raised.

"None whatsoever. You already know how li'l cuz get down. This ain't nothin' new to me."

Phoenix nodded. "And JaMichael, did he tell you why I had you go on this move with him?"

My eyes were closed again. I couldn't look into Phoenix's face. That nigga was so pussy to me. Deep down, I knew he feared what I could really become in any moment. "Nawl, and I don't wanna know. I witnessed it. I took away what I took away from it. Now I just wanna get home and get some sleep. So are we done here?"

Phoenix shook his head. "Nawl, it's best you know why I did what I did. You see, I gave that nigga Scrappy an olive branch to get money under me. He chose to take the blessings that I was giving him to use them in spite of the Duffel Bag Cartel, instead of in favor or in conjunction with. When a nigga say fuck me by doing shit like that, what you saw was the outcome."

Now my eyes were open. "So what you saying, Phoenix? You saying you thank one of dese days that I'm doin' something I ain't supposed to be doing that you gon' send Kool Aid to smoke me?"

Phoenix sat down on the couch. "I hope it never comes to that, because li'l homie ain't gon' play. The game is what it is."

I was fuming, but I had to keep my cards in check and play them close to my chest. "You know what, Phoenix? I respect, honor, and appreciate him too much to cross you. I would never put either of you in that position. It's all family here. I'm Duffel Bag crazy. Let's get money."

Phoenix hopped up. "Now that's what I'm talking about. As long as you keep that sentiment, we gon' be good. I'm the head. You niggas fall under me, and we gon' continue to get rich. Y'all dismissed."

***

Back in the car, while Kool Aid was on the road to dropping me off, I had to get some things off of my chest. So when he was about ten blocks from my pad, I turned to him. "Say Kool Aid, what was all that shit back there with, Phoenix?"

"What are you talking about?" He looked over at me as if he was irritated.

Don't you hate when a ma'fucka tries to fuck you over in some kind of way, and when you confront them about it, they make it seem like they was mad at you? Well, that's the vibe I was getting from, Kool Aid, and that shit was getting me heated. "Nigga, you just took credit for the whole li'l move with Scrappy. You ain't tell that nigga that I saved your ass, or even the fact that we had a few technical difficulties when it came to the move. So what's good?"

"Ain't shit good. That nigga don't need to know everythang, and you didn't save my life. Had you not did what you did, I would have smoked them fools. They were creeping all slow and shit, and I was just playing with Scrappy like a lion does before it devours its prey. That nigga wasn't on shit."

Now ain't this about a bitch! This punk couldn't even give me my props for saving his weak-ass life. Aw, hell nawl! I nodded my head. "Yeah, awright, Kool Aid, that's what's up."

He pulled onto my street and in front of the house. I placed my hand on the handle to the door, and was about to push it open, but I had to get one more thing off of my chest.

"It's been a few of Phoenix traps getting hit all over Orange Mound. That nigga won't admit it, but I heard him talking about it on the phone the other day when he was dropping off a few bricks. Before that nigga Scrappy got smoked, he made it seem like you been knocking off Phoenix's traps. What's good with that?"

Kool Aid looked at me from the corners of his eyes. "That nigga Scrappy was trying to say anything to get up out of that jam. You can't listen to what the fuck he sayin'. You would say anything too if I had that steel to your head."

"You got me fucked up. Ain't no bitches over here, Blood. That nigga would have been stupid to say some shit like that to save his own life. He must've thought that if he reminded you how he'd been holding ya secrets that you wouldn't kill him. I don't know if that was the case, or if you're really hitting that nigga's traps. If you are, do you, but keep that snake shit away from me. Phoenix comes at me with any bullshit, and I'm blowing him down. I don't give a fuck how much of a savage he thank you is. If he come at me with that dumb shit, or if he sends you at me or my shawties, I'ma blow Memphis off the ma'fuckin' map until you niggas slumped. That's on my pops." I opened the door.

"One thang 'bout me, JaMichael, that's that I don't like to be threatened. I already feel like that bitch nigga Scrappy said way too much. Only reason I ain't gon' take shit to the next level with you is because you are my cousin, and I don't see that rat shit in you. If I did, I would have left you back there with Scrappy."

"You thank so?" I asked, closing the door to the car. I'd had enough. I was about to blow his shit out. The last thing I needed was to be worried about this bitch nigga catching me or a member from my household off guard. I wanted to get this shit over and done with right now.

"I say what I mean." He pulled his nose. "But anyway, that shit ain't for me and you. We family."

"We family now, huh?" I adjusted in my seat. My heart was pounding in my chest. I saw myself blowing his brains across the driver's window. I would roll his whip ten blocks down and leave his ass slumped just like that. I'd put a few grams of dope around him and a few loose hundred dollar bills to make that shit look like a robbery. Nawl, scratch that, I'd take pride in cutting his ass up and dumping his parts in the creek. After all, he was family.

"Yeah, I've been hitting Phoenix's traps." He scratched the side of his face. "That nigga eating way more than the rest of us, and the li'l dope and money I be hitting him for ain't gon' hurt his pockets."

I stared at him. I could tell by the facial expressions he made that he really didn't like Phoenix. "Why not just trunk that nigga and take everything that he got? That shit seems like it would be less work?"

Kool Aid smiled. "So what you saying, he doesn't feel any type of way about what I've been doing?"

I opened the passenger's door. "Get money, nigga, just leave me out of that shit. Yo' bidness is yo' bidness, and it is what it is. I'ma fuck wit' you later." I closed the door.

He pulled from in front of the house and stopped the whip. He backed all the way up and stopped in front of the crib again. "Say cuz, my mom's been asking about you like crazy. You need to ride down on her just to make her feel better. Her birthday is next week. Try to at least see her by then. Good night." He threw up the deuces and pulled away.

I stood there for a second until his brake lights disappeared off of the block. I shook my head and looked up at the sky. The stars were shining bright, and the sounds of crickets were close by. Once again, I had gone against my better judgement, and had gotten myself caught up in some bullshit. Instead of being a witness to a bodying session, I had become the one pulling the move. Three murders in one night. Damn, I felt sick. I needed to hold my daughter to ease the pains of the evening. I felt like her energy was the only thing that could both heal me and keep me grounded.

Chapter 11

Three days later, Jahliyah rolled into town riding in a 2020 red Lamborghini truck. It was a warm and breezy day. The sun was shining high in the sky, but it was covered by clouds every so often, before it took the opportunity to peak through them and down to the city of Memphis. I was sitting on our porch sipping from my strawberry lemonade with Jahmya on my lap. The twins were in the yard playing catch with a football. Jahliyah came and parked her truck in front of my house, and because her windows were tinted and I couldn't identify who the whip belonged to, I panicked. I hopped up and ran, Jahmya into the house, and at the same time I called for the boys to come inside. As I was calling them, I was coming off of my waist with a .44 Desert Eagle. They ran past me, and I ran out of the house with my gun leading the way. As I got back to the porch, Jahliyah was coming around the truck, fitted in pink and black Fendi. When she saw me, her face went from a smile to a frown.

I paused in my tracks. "Jahliyah? Fuck."

She lowered her Chanel glasses. "If that ain't my crazy-ass brother. Boy, you ain't changed yet."

I tucked my gun, then rushed down the stairs to pick her up in the air. I spun her around and around. I couldn't believe that she was actually here. Jahliyah was the one female in my life that I loved more than every other one, with the exception of Jahmya. She was my number one. I placed her back on her Chanel pumps. "Sis, why you ain't tell me that you were rolling into Memphis?"

"First of all, I flew in. Secondly, if I had told you, then it wouldn't have been a surprise." She took hold of my hands. "Damn, boy, you look good. You got muscles popping out of everywhere. Why you ain't been on Facebook showing all this shit off? What, you ain't tryna pull in a crazy female fan base for your books?" She rubbed her hand over my chest. "Damn, you got me feeling a way." She blushed.

I moved her hand up off of me and made her slowly turn in a circle. "Shit, look at yo' li'l thick ass. You look like you ten years younger, and ten times finer. Where you been eating from, the fountain of youth?"

She giggled. "Nawl, I'm vegan now, and I work out every single day. You know ever since this real estate empire took off, I have been flying all over the world, and it's a must that I represent my best self. That world is so male dominant and cutthroat, but I do what I gotta do. I'm only in town for one day for a business expo, and I just had to see you and my nephews and niece." She hugged me tight and leaned into my ear. "But we spending a night together tonight. I ain't tryna hear that shit. You looking too good." She backed away and smiled at me. "Now where are the children?"

I pointed to the house and watched her go up the stairs, switching from right to left as she traveled up them. Her Fendi skirt hugged her ass like a second skin. Her thick thighs were popping. One thing for sure and that was that Jahliyah had gotten super bad.

As I was watching her go into the house, a platinum 2020 Bentley Bentayga pulled up right behind Jahliyah's truck. When Bubbie hopped out of the driver's seat, fitted in silver and black Chanel to match the truck, my eyes popped out of my head. She smoked at me and winked. "What's up, baby daddy?" She chirped the alarm.

I frowned and walked up to her as she was dramatically wiping a nonexistent stain off of the bumper of the truck. "Who shit is this?"

"Who do you see driving it?" She smiled devilishly. That's a 2020 Bentley Bentayga. It's a four door hatchback, with twin turbo, eight speed, and the sticker price is a hundred and sixty eight thousand dollars. This ma'fucka is lit, and it's crushing that weak-ass Benz truck you got. Just goes to show you that if a bad bitch wants something done right, then she will do it herself." She snickered and walked past me. "I might have had three kids, JaMichael, but I'm still that bitch. Don't you forget that."

"Shawty, who the fuck bought you this whip?" I grabbed her arm.

"It don't matter. You didn't. Your bag too light. Just like you wanted to cop you a truck, and you did whatever you had to just to get it, well, I did the same thang. A hustler should recognize another hustler. But it look like you feeling salty." She laughed.

I wasn't tripping because she got a truck that was (just keeping shit real) crushing mine. I simply wanted to know where she'd gotten it from. If a nigga was willing to drop some bread like that on a truck for a bitch, he had to have some stupid cash. "Shawty, I applaud yo' hustle. That's what's up. All I wanna know is who bought it for you?"

"Why somebody have to buy it for me? How you know I ain't cop it myself?" She batted her eyelashes.

"Because if you had a hundred and sixty eight thousand dollars, you'd be putting that shit in our bank account because yo' ass is two hundred thousand in arrears from some shit yo' mother got going on. So it looks like we're taking this truck back and getting me my cash. Come on." I pulled her toward it.

She jerked her arm away. "Nigga, let me go. You know damn well I ain't buy this truck. I'm too much of a boss bitch for that." She grunted.

"Then spit that shit out. Which one of these tricking-ass niggas bought it for you?" I stepped into her face.

"Wouldn't you like to know?" She crossed her arms.

"Bubbie, I swear to God, sometimes yo' ass is so childish. Why can't you just answer a simple question?"

"Because it ain't yo' bidness. You're just mad because somebody still sees my worth. You ain't even have the decency to cop me something for holding yo' ass down, yet you go and buy yaself something. Nigga, you selfish, so since didn't I got it done. What you won't do, another nigga always will. Kiss my ass, JaMichael, straight up."

I grabbed her so fast and planted her up against the side of her truck. I held her jaw. "Bubbie, you must really keep forgetting who the fuck I am, ain't you?"

She smacked my hand away. "It doesn't feel so good, do it?"

"What?"

"You keep treating me like a regular bitch, so while you are, in my eyes, you ain't nothing but a regular nigga. I don't give a fuck about what you do, or who you do it with. Just as long as you stay in yo' lane, I'll stay in mine, and that's it. Now get the fuck off of me." She jerked away and made her way upstairs and into the house. She stopped and looked back at me for a moment, then she slammed the door.

***

"What's the matter, li'l bruh? It seems like ever since we been up here you've been acting like you're sick. Do you not wanna be up here with me?" Jahliyah asked, walking in between my legs. She was dressed in a see through purple negligée that had her body looking amazing. She was so thick and so fit at the same time that I couldn't help but to feel a way about her physical presence in front of me. She took my hands and placed them on her ass. "Don't you see all that ass back there?"

I shivered. "Hell yeah, I do."

"Then what's the matter? Don't you know I gotta be on the two o'clock flight tomorrow headed back to New York?" She leaned into my face and rubbed her cheek along the side of mine.

"Yeah, you told me that."

"Well then, what's the matter?" She sat beside me and rubbed her right hand over my stomach muscles.

"Where the fuck, Bubbie get a Bentley truck from? Who she been fuckin' wit'?"

Jahliyah, jerked her head back, and looked at me as if I had lost my mind. "What? Aw, you didn't know?" She raised her eyebrow.

"Didn't know what?" Now I was standing up and looking down at her.

She avoided eye contact with me. "Dang, li'l bruh, why I always gotta be the one to break shit down to you in such a way? We getting too old for this shit."

"You're my ma'fuckin' sister. That's your job!" I snapped.

She exhaled. "Damn. Well, where the fuck do I even begin?" She pulled me back down and wrapped her arm around my neck.

"From the beginning. Don't be leaving shit out either."

"I won't, but before I leave this hotel, we finna get together for old time sake, or I'm finna be extra salty at you." She kissed my lips. "Deal?"

I nodded. Fucking her was the furthest thing from my mind, even though she was smelling good as heaven. "That's a bet."

She exhaled again. "Awright, first things first. After you left, all of your sins came back to haunt Bubbie. Everywhere she travelled around Memphis, she had niggas jumping out on her with guns and threatening to take her life. This was all in the first six months. Did she tell you about any of those incidents?" She eyed me closely. "Of course she didn't, because she told me that she didn't want you stressing in there. Damn, boy. So yeah, there were about five incidents like that, and twice where a group of females actually jumped on her. She almost lost Jahmya, but thank God that she didn't."

I was up and heated. "She ain't tell me about none of that shit. I wonder why she didn't?"

"Because she didn't want you worrying about nothing." She pursed her lips.

I waved her off. "So anyway, how does that amount to her popping up with a Bentley truck?"

"Okay, that's where things get tricky." She ran her fingers through her hair. "Okay, this finna fuck you up. I don't know if you underestimate your woman or not, but that girl is still one of the finest women in Memphis, and now that she done had those kids, and her ass all poked out and shit, she really a sight for sore eyes."

"Man, fuck all that shit, Jahliyah. Who she fuckin' wit'? You 'bout to have me choke yo' ass out."

Jahliyah stood up. "Before I tell you anythang, you gon' have to sit down." She grabbed my shoulders and led me to the bed, where I took a seat. "Okay, bruh, now don't snap out, just listen."

Chapter 12

"When you left, like I said, plenty niggas got to coming at her because of the shit that you've done to them. You already know how most bitch niggas get down in Memphis. They got a tendency of taking the easy way out. They'd rather sweat a nigga's woman instead of the nigga himself, and that's just what they did to your woman. So since she was defenseless and didn't have a protector out here, Kool Aid stepped in and I guess they was fuckin' around for a minute, but I'm not sure. Bubbie never did confirm or deny if they did or not." She waited to see what kind of an effect this would have on me. "You okay?"

I nodded. "Yeah, go on."

"Well, that nigga Kool Aid ain't nothing but a stick-up kid. He don't know how to get to the paper like you did, so you should already know that he couldn't be a replacement for you. Then her mother got into some financial difficulties with the Feds, and that's when Bubbie knew that she had to step her game up. So she got a temporary job at one of cousin Phoenix's strip clubs as a bottle girl. That's where she met Bagg, and she been rocking wit' him, and those Bread Gang niggas ever since then. Bagg smitten by your baby mama, and he be spoiling that girl. He's the only reason that there is money in y'all's bank account right now because Bubbie's mother, Yvonne, had cleaned it out."

I lowered my head and tried my best to process everything. "Damn, so you're basically saying that she did fuck off on me while I was locked down?"

Jahliyah shrugged her shoulders. "It was five years, li'l bruh. Do you honestly think that you could have held her down for five years without fuckin' somebody else?"

"It ain't even about that, Jahliyah, and you know it." I walked over to the wall and rested my hand on it. "But it's good though. I already figured that her and Kool Aid had something going on. I just hate imagining that shit. But now she fuckin' rappers and all that shit? Don't she know them ma'fuckas be smashing hoes all over the world? Damn, and I ate her pussy and shit. I feel disgusted."

Jahliyah laughed. "Boy, stop it. Now you're doing too much. You know damn well that girl done washed her cat more than a thousand times before she let you put your mouth down there. Now come here, baby. Damn, I need you." She slowly walked over to me and slid her arms around my neck. She placed her forehead against mine. "I'm saying, I know you got some shit you gotta figure out with your baby mama and all that, but tonight you're with your sister, and I ain't seen you physically like this in years. So I'm just saying, can we do this for old time's sake, or what?" She kissed my lips and licked all over them.

I reached out and grabbed her ass. Now that I knew Bubbie had did this thing while I was locked, I felt like I was free to fuck somethin', and I had plans on getting a whole lot of pussy based off the dumb shit that she had done. "I been wanting to fuck you my whole life. When I was shaggy, you had a habit of playing wit' me and teasing and shit 'cause I was your little brother, but I ain't going for that shit now. I gotta have this thick ass." I was squeezing all over that juicy-ass booty, all under it and in the crease. Jahliyah wasn't wearing no panties, and her pussy was hot and already moist. I bit into her neck.

"Mmm, JaMichael. I never meant to tease you. I was just scared. I knew we shouldn't ever cross those lines. And I was the oldest. It was my job to watch over you. But you best believe, I always wanted to give you the pussy. I was just

scared. How would that have made you look at me right now?"
She leaned her head all the way back and moaned.

My lips sucked up and down her neck. She smelled so
good. "That shit would have let me know that you loved me.
Every nigga in America that got a bad-ass sister like you
would love to take her ass down. Them niggas just won't
admit that shit in public. But fuck them. This is us." I picked
her up and carried her to the bed. Her thick thighs wrapped
around my waist. When we got to the bed I laid her back, and
pushed her negligée upward and around her stomach.

She curled her back and spaced her thighs. "Damn, li'l
bruh, are we really finna do this shit?"

"Hell yeah, we is." My face snuck into her crease. I
separated her pussy lips and sniffed her box hard.

"Unnnh," she groaned and opened her thighs wider.

"Baby bruh 'bout to break yo' ass down. Watch this
shit." I licked up and down her crease over and over again
before my tongue ran circles around her clitoris.

"Uh! Uh! Uh! Baby bruh, oooh, shit." She grabbed my
head and wrapped her slim ankles around my neck.

I really went crazy then. I licked and sucked and flicked
my tongue as fast and as firm as I could. Every time she
squealed, I got a better grip on her pearl tongue with my lips
and sucked as if it was a nipple.

This really sent her over the edge. Jahliyah sat up on her
hands and started to scream at the top of her lungs. She
humped into my mouth, and then fell to the bed, bucking up
into it over and over. "I'm cumming! Fuck! I'm cumming,
baby bruh!" She opened her thighs super wide and rubbed her
clit while my tongue attacked her nub every chance I got.
Finally she began to shake and push me away.

I grabbed her by the ankle while I pulled my boxers off
of me. I kicked them off and rushed to get between her thighs.

She rubbed all over my chest. Her hands wound up between my legs. She gripped me in her right palm, closed her fingers, and proceeded to pump me.

"I wanna see you cum, li'l bruh. I wanna see you cum so bad." She stuck two fingers into herself and smeared her juices all around my piece. Her scent was so intoxicating, both loud and forbidden. That shit was right up my alley. She crawled onto her knees. She pushed me onto my back and took hold of my piece again. As soon as I was positioned in her hand, she kissed the big head. Then she licked it, opened her mouth wide, and sucked me into it before closing her lips around the head and sucking me like a porn star. "Unh!" She popped me out. "This what I been wanting to do ever since we were kids." She started sucking again for two straight minutes.

I lay there going crazy, making sounds that I'm ashamed to admit that I made. The harder and faster she sucked me, the louder I got. All of my fantasies that I'd had of her when we were kids came to the forefront of my brain. Even the ones where she'd play with her coochie next to me when we were younger and she thought that I was asleep. Every time I closed my eyes, I got so close to cumming that I had to catch myself and open them. I pushed her away. My dick popped out of her lips and a loud sucking noise emitted.

"Aww, what are you doing, baby brother? I was just getting used to sucking this dick."

I stood up on my knees stroking my piece while I watched her rub her pussy, slowly yet deliberately. That made me harder. "Fuck that. Every time we went down this path before we always stopped before I could hit the pussy. Well, not this time. Bend that fat-ass booty over and get on them knees. I want this shit doggy style. You are too ma'fuckin' thick now."

She moaned and assumed the position. She pulled her negligée up to her waist and spaced her knees. "Come get this pussy, li'l bruh. I know you've been wanting to hit this shit."

She wasn't lying. Out of all of the females that I had fantasized about while I was on lock, Jahliyah was the only one that I could really cum from while I was having my solo sessions, and that's only because me and her had done so much freaky shit as kids. But no matter what we did, she never did let me fuck. And that was the most irritating part of our whole childhood for me. Because we had done everything but that.

I got behind her and rubbed my dick head up and down her slit. She was dripping wet. The lips were hot and spongy. I rubbed all over her caramel ass before slowly sliding into her inch by inch. "Fuck, Jahliyah."

She balled the sheets into her hand and arched her back. "Unnnnh shit, you're finally about to fuck me." She moved backward and helped me to impale my piece inside of her deeper.

I grabbed a hold of her hips and watched my dick separate her chocolate lips before I slid all the way in. I slapped her on the ass and moaned with my heart looking down at our connection. I gripped that juicy booty meat, and then I got to fucking her like there was no tomorrow. "Gimme this shit! Gimme this shit! Fuck! Shit! Unh! Unh! Unh!" I crashed into her over and over again.

Jahliyah opened her mouth wide and laid the left side of her face on the bed. "Aww! Aww! JaMichael! Uhhhh fuck! JaMichael! Fuck me! Fuck me! Fuck sis! Fuck me!" She pushed back into me over and over.

My eyes rolled into the back of my head. The forbidden aspect of it all, mixed with how wet and tight her pussy was, became too much, too soon. I slapped her ass and hollered out before cumming all in her, jerking like crazy. "Huh! Huh! Huh! Huhhhhhhhhhh!" I groaned, nutting like I had never nutted before.

Jahliyah popped her ass into my lap over and over, milking me. Then she pulled her pussy off of me, turned all the way around, and proceeded to pump me at full speed before she sucked me into her mouth until she felt me harden again.

She peered up at me with that devilish look in her eyes, her hand working magic on my pipe. "You should have already known that you couldn't trust no bitch, JaMichael. If it's one thing that I always tried to instill in you, it's that you can't trust no female–other than me." Sue sucked me back into her mouth and slurped me for five straight minutes while she rubbed all over my stomach and chest. Then she pushed me backward and climbed atop me. She bit into my neck. "Damn, I love you so much. I hate when you're hurting. Lord knows I hate when my little brother is hurting." She reached behind herself and slid me back into her gap, took a hold of my shoulders once she sank all the way down, and proceeded to ride me loudly with her head thrown back. Her pretty titties bounced up and down on her chest. Her tongue circled her lips. She let out sexual moans that caused ripples to go through me. "Tell me you love me, JaMichael. Tell me." She huffed and puffed.

My hands were running all over her ass. Jahliyah was strapped. "I love you. Fuck. I love you, girl."

She growled and leaned down so that her face was in my neck. Once there, she bit and sucked all over it. "Ain't nobody gon' do you like me. Don't no bitch love you like I do." She moaned. "Shit." She kissed my lips while slamming into me harder and harder.

I groaned and rolled her over. My piece slipped out. I got aggressive. I pushed her knees to her shoulders and slipped back in after a little maneuvering. Then I got to fucking her so hard that I couldn't help letting out noises myself.

"Unnnn! Unnnn! Unnnn! Baby bruh, shit. Wait! Wait! Aww shit, baby! Unnnn!" She screamed and came, falling to the bed with her body jerking like crazy.

I dug and dug until it got so good that I couldn't take any more. I folded her all the way up and slammed home deep. "Shit, Jahliyah, dis pussy fye'! Uhhhh! Uhhhh! Uhhhh!" I splashed all in that cave over and over, twitching like something was wrong with me. The feeling kept getting better and better until my piece got sensitive and I had to back up. I rolled on to my back and laid there breathing hard.

Jahliyah crawled around and took a hold of my dick again. She sucked it into her mouth, looking me in the eyes. She took it out and stroked it. "Don't you ever depend on those other bitches, JaMichael. I got you. Don't think that just because I'm traveling that you aren't still my number one priority, and I'll drop anything for you whenever you need me, because I will. All you gotta do is let me know what you need." She kissed the top of my head and sucked me back into her mouth again, bobbing her head for two minutes, then she climbed up my body, straddled me, and closed her eyes.

***

Thirty minutes later, I was still laid up with Jahliyah. I was both tired and exhausted, but my brain wouldn't allow my mind to stop racing. I kept imagining Bubbie with that Bagg nigga, and even Kool Aid. I tried my best to replay my entire incarceration over in my mind's eye and all of the times of dealing with her, and I swear looking back, I never saw any chinks in her armor or had any reason to believe that she was fucking off with another nigga or cheating. I think it's because whenever I needed her to do something, she jumped on it ASAP. I had never needed for anything for as long as I had been down. Second to that, she was always available. Whenever I called her, she picked up. I don't give a fuck what time of the day or night it was, she picked up. Because of all of those things, I thought I would be able to tell her level of faithfulness, but I guess I was wrong. As heartless as I was, that thought shattered me on so many levels.

Jahliyah rolled from on top of me and scooted in front of me, placing her ass in my lap. She grabbed my arm and made me place it around her body. "Go to sleep, JaMichael. I can tell something is bothering you. You gotta let it go." She yawned. "Please, because it's worrying my spirit."

"I'm trying to sis, I swear to Jehovah, I am. But it's fucking with me."

"What, that girl? I mean yo' baby mama dilemma?" She looked back at me.

"Yeah."

She yawned again and rolled all the way around until she was facing me. She placed her small hand on the side of my face. "Aww, baby, you can't allow what another person does to bring you down. All you can do as a man is to keep moving forward and do everything that you are supposed to do for your family and even her. Sex is just that – sex. Don't make it out to be more than what it is. Everybody fucks. It's not a big deal. Now come on, let's go to sleep." She placed her forehead against mine and held the back of my neck.

I closed my eyes, but no sleep came to me. On the one hand, Jahliyah, was right. Sex was just sex, but that only became truth when you didn't actually care about the other person that was fucking. It was something else when you loved that person, and you trusted that person, and you didn't see anything like that coming. Also, a man finds himself trying to play back all of the times that she could have been involved with another person, and I was asking myself where were the signs, and how did she act in front of me? I honestly couldn't find any. That is what was messing with my head more than anything else. I got to thinking so hard that I wound up giving myself a migraine. Then and only then was I able to drift off to sleep, and it was with a mug on my face.

Jahliyah flew back to New York the next afternoon after we got it in one more time. By the time she left, I was physically exhausted, and mentally, even worse. As I watched her plane fly away it was like all of my realities came at me from every angle to the point I felt broken and angry. I knew I had to get to the bottom of what had taken place ever since I was gone, and every time something was revealed, I would get my sadistic revenge. That, I knew, was the only thing that would make me feel better.

Ghost

Chapter 13

Two days later, I woke up one morning to Bubbie singing happily while she sat at her vanity table in our bedroom combing her hair. I sat up, rubbed my eyes, yawned, and looked over at her. She looked happy and cheerful as she continued to do her thing with her eyes fixed on herself in the mirror. I got out of the bed and stepped over to her after adjusting my manhood, which never wanted to lay down in the morning.

She looked up to me through the reflection in the mirror. "Good morning, handsome. How did you sleep last night?"

"Awright. Where did you sleep?" I asked, yawning again. Ever since our argument about the Benz truck, she and I never slept in the bed at the same time. If I was there first, she would come in, grab a few articles of clothing, and leave back out to find another room in the house to sleep in. Whenever I found her there, I would fall into the bed beside her. She would then get up and leave.

"I slept with the boys last night. I figured you'd snatch up Jahmya, as you usually did, but you'd ignore their room, as usual. So yeah." She started to hum to herself again, brushing her hair.

"You tryna say that I am ignoring my sons or somethin'?" I felt offended.

"Dang, before you get all on my nerves and shit this morning, can you at least go and brush your teeth? Don't shit on me." She frowned.

"Man, as many times as you have woke up on some lovey dovey shit first thang in the morning with your breath smelling some type of way, you really finna try and go there with me?"

She rolled her eyes. "When people are in love, their breath doesn't stank to each other."

I came closer to her and squatted directly by her. I didn't care what my breath was smelling like. It didn't taste funny or nothing. "So what, you saying you don't love me no more?"

"JaMichael, I don't feel like arguing with yo' strong-looking ass. Damn, it's eight o'clock in the morning."

I was hurt. I walked into the bathroom and handled my hygiene before I came out with a heavy heart. She was putting the finishing touches on her hair. I came beside her again needing clarity. "Bubbie, are you saying you don't love me anymore?"

"Here we go." She sighed and rolled her eyes again. "JaMichael, why do we have to keep going through this? Damn, can't you see I'm trying to get ready?"

"Get ready? Where you think you finna go?"

She snickered. "I know you done lost yo' damn mind asking me something like that. You definitely lost that privilege." She turned her back to me and pulled the closet door open.

I appeared behind her. "So you think that just because we're on rocky terms right now it gives you the right to do whatever you wanna do?"

"Boy, you are the last one that should be saying some shit like that. You come and go as you please, and I don't say anything. You walk around here like you own the place, and once again, I don't say anything. You favor your daughter, and neglect your twins, and I still don't say anything. I let you do you, and I expect for you to let me do me. But now that you're stepping on what I'm trying to do, we got a problem."

"Why you can't answer the ma'fuckin' question? Do you love me or not?"

She lowered her head. "You know what? Yeah, I love you, JaMichael. You are my first love, the father to my three beautiful children, so yeah, I love you. Are you happy now?" She bumped me out of the way and grabbed a hanger that had a Prada blouse on it.

"Nawl, shawty, I ain't talking that watered down ass love. I mean do you love me like I'm your man?"

"You mean am I in love with you?" She raised her left eyebrow.

"Yeah, that?"

"Boy, nawl. She grunted. "I hate you right now. If I was a man, I'd kick yo' ass all up and down Memphis. You're disrespectful, you're disloyal, you're not showing the signs of a good father, and you make me feel like shit. So nawl, how could I be in love with a man like that?"

"How am I not a good father? I make sure all the bills are taken care of around here. Our children have everything that they need and want. We live in a big house, three whips. What more do you want from me?"

"When was the last time that you spent a day alone with your boys? Huh? When was the last time you threw a football or bounced a basketball with them? Seriously? Have you ever done it? Because to my knowledge, you have not." She ran her fingers through her hair. "You love Jahmya, we all get that, but it seems that she is the only person in this family that you do love." She stopped and exhaled loudly.

Damn, had I been neglecting my sons and favoring Jahmya more than anybody else in the family? I stopped and replayed my day by day since I'd gotten out. The more and more I thought about it, Bubbie was right. "That's gon' change starting today. I'ma take them wherever they wanna go and spend a bag on them. You can watch Jahmya. That way she doesn't get in the way of what I am supposed to do for them. Bet?"

"JaMichael, the kids are gone with my mother for the weekend. I told you this yesterday." She cut her eyes at me. "But when they do get back, why don't you take some time to get to know them? You'll find more reasons to love them with every conversation. After all, they are yours." She started to walk away.

I grabbed her arm lightly. "Bubbie." I turned her around until she was facing me.

"What, JaMichael?"

"Baby, I love you with all of my heart, and I'm so, so sorry for fucking up since I been home. I been down a minute, and this freedom thing is taking some getting used to. When I left, I was a new father. I never got the experience that I needed to actually be this amazing father that you have always wanted me to be, but just give me a chance, please."

"JaMichael, if you loved your sons as much as you do that little girl, who looks so much like yo' ass, then everything would be awright. You got it in you. You're just gender bias."

"Okay then, I'll do a better job." I pulled her to me and hugged her waist. "How can I get right with you though?"

She was quiet for a moment, avoiding my eyes. "I don't know."

I smiled. "Come on, baby, don't be like that. Tell me. I'm willing to do anything."

"Why all of a sudden now, huh? Why didn't you ask me this a month ago?" Bubbie snapped, wiggling out of my embrace.

"I don't know why then, but I'm asking you now. Look, I don't wanna lose you. I love you with all of my heart, and love makes no sense without you. I'm willing to do whatever I gotta do to get things right with you. That's how I feel, and

I need for you to come up to my level. We got a whole family to think about."

"Ain't dis 'bout a BITCH!" She backed all the way up, and looked me up and down. "You got the nerve to bring this family shit out of your mouth, when it seems like you've been about everything other than that. I don't know who you're fuckin' in those streets, but it shows that you're doing something because your whole-ass demeanor has changed. Nigga, I can tell that you don't wanna be in this house with me and these kids. That's why I'm starting to resent yo' selfish ass. Got the nerve to pop three babies in me and thank he can go off and running the streets as if he ain't got a whole-ass family at home to get his ass back to. Boy, I should punch you in your throat. Where is your loyalty?"

"Loyalty? That's really the word you used? Seriously?" I laughed.

"Sure did."

I stepped into her face. "When you start fucking wit' Bagg?"

She dropped her head. "And we're back to this. JaMichael, you used to play his music all day before you got locked up, and since you been home - that is, until you found out that he and I are friends. Now, all of the sudden, he's a bitch-ass nigga, and we can't play his music, and you wanna know how he and I came to be cool."

"Fuck cool. Was you getting smashed by that nigga when I was on lock and did you fuck Kool Aid?"

She frowned. "Nigga, didn't I tell yo' simple ass that I have never cheated on you while you were down?"

"Yeah, you did, but that ain't what the streets are saying."

"Fuck the streets. The streets can't tell you what I did behind closed doors. And to answer your question, no, I never fucked Kool Aid, or Bagg, while you were locked down. On my kids, I was extremely loyal to you. Ain't no nigga touched this pussy. I am more of a woman than to cheat on my man while he's jammed up. Damn, why would you get me pregnant if you thought you were seeding a whore's womb?" She pushed me away from her. "Move." She sprayed perfume on to her neck, wrist, and up and down her midsection before putting on her blouse. "You got some nerve."

I stood there not knowing if I believed her or not, but I was honestly leaning toward the way of that I did. After all, she had put it on our children. "Wait a minute, you said you didn't cheat while I was locked down. What about now?"

She pulled up her Prada jeans with a bit of a struggle. They conformed to her ass. She fastened the button and slipped a Prada belt into the loops. "Aw, you see now it's open season. You got out on pure bullshit. You ain't did shit that I thought you were going to do, so now I'm doing me. So nawl while you were locked, ain't shit move, but now that you're home and I see this is what it is. I'm about to live my best life." She grabbed her Chanel frames and slipped them on to her face. She sat on the edge of the bed and placed her freshly pedicured feet inside of some tan Chanel pumps with a blue bottom, then she stood up. "Nigga, if you want me, you're going to have to fight for me and earn me back, 'cause I gotta be honest with you, while you're in trenches getting money for another nigga's Cartel, I'm messing with Bagg and the Bread Gang real tough, and contrary to his raps, he treats me like a ma'fuckin' Queen. This is Memphis. He knows that. We both bleed this city."

"Shawty, don't be telling me 'bout no other nigga. You gon' get bruh's ass whacked. That's on my shawties."

"Oh yeah? You mean to tell me that you're jealous? With all of those women over there willing to drop their government-issued panties for you at the drop of a hat?" She gave me a goofy face. "Nawl, not you." She laughed.

I started feeling like a sucka. "Check dis shit out, Bubbie. You my bitch, and you ain't fuckin' wit' no other nigga but me. That shit wit' Bagg, and whoever else, is dead. Now play wit' it if you want to."

"First of all…" She pointed her finger in my face, "I ain't yours, or nobody else's, bitch. I got three kids. I am a mother first, and a queen second. You need to check yo'self, and grow the fuck up." She pushed my head with her finger. "Secondly, what yo' punk ass won't do, another nigga will. You don't wanna give me the emotional support that I need, then I'll go find somebody that does. You don't wanna be here for me mentally, and help me care for these children totally, and not only in thirds, then I will go find somebody that will. I don't need a boy, JaMichael. I gotta have a man, and that's what I'm locking down right now. When you decide to grow up, then we can come back to the table to see where that leaves us, but for right now, you and I are nothing more than co-parents staying under the same roof. I ain't on that with you right now."

"Yeah, Bubbie?"

"Yeah, JaMichael. I don't care about you getting mad either. Suck it up. You fucked us up. Now do whatever you wanna do but stay in yo' lane. I got this." She picked up her Bentley keys and chirped her truck's alarm. "Don't wait up." She grabbed her Dooney and Burke bag before leaving out of the bedroom. Then she stopped in her tracks. "And in reference to Kool Aid, I mean, since we are putting it all out there. I feel a way about him because he protected me while you were gone. We almost went there a few times while you were in lock, but we didn't - I didn't, I should say. But once again, you're home now, so all of that loyalty for no reason shit is off the table. Phoenix wasn't on his best behavior either, and he ain't ever been since you been back. Might as well run the gambit, right? Yeah, later, boy." She winked at me, then left.

  I stood there fuming. For as long as I had been alive, I had never been angrier. My eyes watered, and my heart was pounding so hard in my chest that I felt like I couldn't breathe. I finally sat on the edge of the bed and allowed for the tears to fall from my eyes. I didn't even know what I was crying about, but I did it for a full thirty minutes. After that, I stood up and was good.

Chapter 14

"Mane, ever since you've been home, the traps have been jumping harder than ever in Black Haven. I don't know what you be doing, but I gotta applaud your genius." Phoenix said this and scooted a pile of cash in front of me.

I picked it up and set it on my lap, counting it hundred dollar bill for hundred dollar bill. "I just do what I do."

We were sitting in the den of his safe house. There was a red light bulb screwed into the socket, so the ambiance was all blood-like. He had two stuffed duffel bags of cash beside him and a Draco across his lap. There was a big blunt burning in his lips, and we were both sippin on codeine.

"I got this shipment of this new shit coming in by the boatload at the end of the week. The ma'fuckas down south of the border swearing up and down that it's gon' turn the city out. I'm tryna flood Memphis, and Harris County too. Them Texas folk love eating out of the palm of the Duffle Bag Cartel. The sales are starting to compete with the ones out here. I can't complain. As long as the money keeps coming, that's all that really matters. You feel me?"

I took a sip of my drank. "Yeah, nigga, I feel you." I imagined him coming at Bubbie bogusly, and then myself knocking his shit back. A creepy smile spread across my lips. "So how much of this shit is coming to Black Haven?"

"Fifty bricks. I'm putting it all in your lap so you can handle yo' bidness. You thank you can shuffle it?"

I grabbed my blunt out of the ashtray and puffed off of it. "Hell yeah, that shit light. Don't forget how I used to have Orange Mound jumping back in the day."

"I remember - you know, after you took it from me and shit." He lowered his eyes and frowned.

I held up my bottle. "Yeah, that was the past. We gotta leave that shit back there."

Phoenix mugged me for a minute. "Yeah, right." His eyes never left my face.

"Nigga, why the fuck you keep staring at me?"

"What was going through your mind back in the day when you came at me? Why didn't you see us as family, and treat me as such?"

"What?" I laughed and looked off. "Man, Phoenix, get off of that soft-ass shit. When we bumped heads back in the day, there was too much shit going on with both you and your mans Mikey. My sister had been kidnapped and abused, and you were too close to everything for my liking. How the fuck could I embrace you when I thought you had something to do with her abduction? That shit doesn't make no sense."

"But I told you I didn't. You should have honored that shit." He placed his blunt in the ashtray.

"Fuck what you talking about. That's my sister. I wasn't finna embrace no nigga that I felt could have hurt her until I knew for sure they were clear. Then when it came to taking over Orange Mound, that was just the spoils of war. A savage is what a savage is, and I came for the homeland. You did what you had to do to survive. You eventually got it back. It worked out for the greater good of you, I guess."

Phoenix stood up. "So what you saying? Are you saying that back then if I hadn't turned over the hood to you that you would have killed me?"

I stood up now. I took four more puffs off of my blunt and inhaled them bitches. "Nigga, I would have killed you, and every Duffle Bag Cartel nigga I could find, fuck all of the bitches in their family, and put 'em down with the Heartless Goons. How does that sound to you?" I stubbed out my blunt.

Phoenix held his Draco, shaking a bit. "Li'l dawg, I swear to God, if you weren't my cousin, I would blow your brains out."

I upped my burner off of my waist and cocked it. "Act like I ain't then, Phoenix. Bitch nigga, do what you feel like doing and I'm finna splatter this den wit' our blood. Fuck family. Move sum'."

Phoenix slowly backed up and cocked the Draco on the side. I already had my mind set that as soon as he raised his arm I was bucking his ass down immediately and with no hesitation. He placed his finger on the trigger with a mug on his face, then he busted up laughing.

I was shaking, ready to kill something. I didn't know what was so funny. I definitely didn't get the joke. "Fuck so funny?"

He pointed at me. "You, dawg. There is something seriously wrong with you. You were ready to blow me down for real wasn't you?"

I kept my silence. I needed to see what angle he was coming from. Was he serious before? Was he just trying to get a rise out of me? What was he up to?

"Look JaMichael…" He ushered for me to sit down on the couch. I sat. He placed the Draco on the couch beside him and grabbed his drink. He looked over at me. "Man, I don't have anything against you. I know we had a shady past, but that's over now. We both got families. We gotta do better and get as much money as we can before the game consumes us. All I need to know is that I can trust him to let that old shit go. Can you continue to function with me as the head, or are we going to have a major problem down the road?"

I would never expose my hand to this nigga. I didn't give a fuck how he tried to finesse me. The bottom line was that I didn't like his punk ass, cousin or not, and I was used to being head of my own thing. "Nawl, we shouldn't have no problems, cuz. I got mad love for you, and I ain't got no ill feelings in my heart. I let that shit go five years back, but that doesn't mean that there is any hoe in me. I know who you are, and what you represent, but I am still a man, and I will not be stood on by nobody - not even you. So while we won't have any problems, that doesn't mean that we ain't gon' butt heads from time to time. As long as I keep the money flow coming for you, we should be able to get past that though."

"And we will. We most definitely will. We're blood, family fights, but we make up and remember that blood is thicker than water. As long as you got me, I got you. Now go 'head and count yo' cash. Let me know what your final total is, and tell me what you think about the raise I just gave you?" He sat back on the couch and smiled. It turned to a frown quickly. "Some nigga been knocking off my traps every other week or so. I lost every bit of a half a mill in products and cash. I wanted to hit you a little more but shit a little funny in a few areas right now. But what can you really do?" He took another sip from his codeine and closed his eyes. "Tell you what doe, I ever find out who got enough balls to rob me, I'ma make shit real difficult for 'em. I'm talking I'ma get rid of they whole family. The world'll be a better place if it wasn't for so many rats and turn coats. Not saying I don't understand the whole stick-up kid side of thangs, just don't like being on the receiving end, and I can't accept it." He laid back on the couch, his eyes remained closed.

I scooted to the edge of the sofa that I was sitting on and looked him over. I could tell that he was turnt all the way up. His speech was starting to slow down, and his fingers couldn't stay still. His bottom lip quivered just a bit, and he kept trying his best to swallow his spit - with no success, I imagined. "Say, bruh?"

He opened his eyes. "What's to it?"

"You talking all dis shit about losing money and all of that. What you finna do, lay down and roll over while some off-brand nigga capitalizes off of all of the hard work that we be doing in this cartel? What type of shit is that?" I needed to gas him up as much as possible, because the madder he got, or the more bitch he felt like, the higher he would drive up the bounty on the person's head that was ripping him off. Niggas in power were so see through.

He scooted forward on his couch, just as I had, and wiped his mouth. "Mane, you damn sho' barking on something. But what the fuck more can I do? I already got Kool Aid scouring the city looking for any nobody-ass niggas that look like they done came up on a nice piece of change. I got my hittas with their ear to the street, and the best I can do right now."

I shook my head. "Nawl, you fuckin' up, cuz. You fuckin' up big time, and you don't even see it." I fell back after grabbing my blunt out of the ashtray and sparking it.

Phoenix sat there for a moment in deep thought. Then he nodded his head to me. "What you talkin 'bout?"

I laughed shortly. "The way I see it, if a nigga got enough heart to rob your traps, Phoenix, it's only because he thinks that you are sweet. He doesn't honor your gangsta, and he doesn't honor the Duffel Bag Cartel. Niggas like that are predators. They do small things at first just to see how much they can get away with. But the more they do get away, the more emboldened they become. Before you know it, whoever doing this will have formed a crew to flat out take over the Cartel properties and clientele. Seeing as the Duffel Bag Cartel is what's feeding me and my kin, I ain't 'bout to sit back and let dis shit happen like that bruh. All I need to know is, what is the reward for me finding the culprit or culprits?"

Phoenix stood up on wobbly legs. "Mane, you find da nigga dat thank I'm so sweet, and 'tween me and you, it's a million dollars in it for you. That's a million in cash. On my cartel, I'll pay you soon as you brang his ass before me."

I nodded and rubbed my hands together. "What about a piece of Black Haven too? You know, not enough to step outside of the Duffle Bag Cartel or nothing like that, but a few projects so that I can see what it feels like to have my crew up under me. Of course my loyalty will still be to the Duffel Bag Cartel, but my troops would answer to me. But we'd still be under you."

"If that's the case, why not leave shit the way that it is? I mean, you're eating and getting money and all of that. Why would you fuck with the fabric of what we got going on?"

"Come on, Phoenix. You already know how shit is. Every man wants his own army for himself. I ain't no different." I took a sip from my codeine to make it look light with what I was talking about, even though I was dead serious. I kept a slight smile on my face.

"Nawl, mane, that shit dead. You gon' be Duffel Bag Cartel, or I gotta crush you. That's what that is. If you find this nigga that's doing this shit to my Cartel, and you bring him to me, I got a million dollars for you in cash, and whatever kind of truck you want. I already bought yo' bitch a Bentley truck just for being so stomp down while you were gone. It won't be nothing to buy you one and the same. I got the dealerships all across Memphis sewed up." He popped his collar and nodded his head.

"Wait a minute. You bought her that truck?" I stood up. "I thought that Bagg nigga from the Bread Gang bought it for her.

"He promised me three shows at my club that's opening next month, and in exchange, he wanted the truck for Bubbie

122

and a half brick of coke. I made it happen, but he was still way short. I took it upon myself to walk her onto the lot and cop that truck for her. She said she needed it, and when a woman needs something, you gotta make sure you deliver right away." He rubbed his chin. "Shawty still got the game."

I nodded. "Yeah, she sho' do." I grabbed my pistol off of the table and tucked it into the small of my back. "I'm about to hit up the slums to see what I can find out about your traps. Then I'ma head over to Black Haven and get to it." I grabbed an empty duffel bag that was next to the couch and proceeded to stuff my cash into it. I would count it later. My mind was racing too bad to do it now.

"Yeah, you do that. For the record, that's a hunnit thousand in that bag. It's just a little token of my appreciation, don't even mention it, and consider it a bonus. It ain't got nothing to do with what you got coming at the end of the week."

"Bet those. Before I go. What's really to them Bread Gang niggas? They connected to this cartel or what?"

"If it ain't got Duffel Bag in front of it, then it ain't got no connection to us. Fuck every other gang, cartel, or ma'fucka that's trying to infiltrate this mob." He rubbed the side of his Draco. "I don't know, man, they mostly made up of rappers and a few dope boys. Most of them come from the jungle, but don't we all? Why, what's up wit' it?"

"And Bagg, what up wit' him?"

"He got the rap game right now. He seeing a few M's, but that doesn't mean he can't be touched. What, you feeling some type of way about him and Bubbie or something?" A smirk came across his face.

I wouldn't dare give him the satisfaction. "Nawl, I just wanted to know who she be having around my kids," I lied. But ain't that every nigga's response when he feeling jaded?

Phoenix laughed. "You got a bad bitch, JaMichael. You already know what happens to bad hoes in Memphis?"

"Nawl, shawty, what happen to dem?"

"They get fucked and bagged. If that pussy good, they get Bentley trucks. If it ain't, they get kicked to the curb or put up in strip clubs where they can fool goofies. Only the bosses truly know what that thang like." He laughed. "I'ma holler, boy, go get money."

Chapter 15

"Mane, that nigga just dropped off eighty kilos to the Mound, and word on the street is that he didn't have to pay shit up front. Those Mexicans down in Mexico City is fronting him the work. That means that it's eighty bricks in the Mound, fifty in Black Haven, and he still got damn near ten million dollars in cash spread all around his traps," I said as I rolled through Black Haven with Kool Aid sitting in the passenger's seat.

Kool Aid had a Visine bottle half-filled with water, and the other half with heroin. He shook it up, and every so often he would snort a drip of it. He was leaning all the way on the door with his eyes partly closed. "Say potna, yo' numbers are slightly off, but you said all of this to say what?"

"I'm saying that right now the getting is good. Now is the time for you to handle yo' bidness and get yo' bands all the way up." I hit a corner and rolled down the long strip of the projects. The sun was just beginning to set on a warm day. The area was crowded with both women scantily clad and dope boys hustling to the max. I'd already dropped off more than a few packages for distribution, and all I had to do now was sit back and let them catch that bread.

"I already know that you really didn't give me the go ahead one way or the other, but you coming at me with this bit of enthusiasm is throwing me off. What made you change yo' tune so tough to come over here and support my endeavors? You find out that nigga Phoenix fucking Bubbie?"

I was stuck for a moment. I knew that my next response and move had to be my best move. "Dat ain't my bidness. Shawty is a grown woman. All we do is take care of our kids together, and besides, I gave Phoenix the go ahead," I lied. "He came and asked me like a man."

Kool Aid sat up and looked over at me. "Yeah? That nigga had enough gall to do that?" He looked me over.

"Yup."

"Damn, I know you had to be fucked up behind that question. I could have never asked you no shit like that. I figure the best policy is don't ask, don't tell. Bubbie a ma'fucka though. Damn, she so strapped."

"Yeah, she's straight. But anyway, what 'bout what I was running by you?"

"You talking 'bout me breaking his shit off? Aw, I'm still gon' keep doing that. But how is that going to benefit you at all? Seems pointless for you to be so amped up about it." He grabbed his Tech Nine from under his seat and placed it on his lap. "Never did like Black Haven Projects. It's some grimy ma'fuckas like me over here." He pulled his Coronavirus mask over his nose.

I kept scrolling. I handed him my phone. "Check these three addresses right here. I just personally dropped off ten bricks to each one, and Phoenix is supposed to be doubling back tomorrow to pick up fifty G's apiece from each spot. That's a hunnit and fifty bands. Hit these ma'fuckas tonight, and it's good. "

Kool Aid looked at the phone. "Yeah, dese ma'fuckas right here?" He smiled. "You still ain't told me what's in it for you?"

"On some real shit, I got a few tricks up my sleeve. I can't see myself being under Phoenix for the rest of my hustling career. I got to make a few moves and then I'ma emerge."

Kool Aid's eyes got big. "Damn, you finna bring back them Heartless Goon niggas, ain't you?"

I avoided his eye contact. "Would you come and fuck with me if I did? You know, if I made sure that you stayed with a bag every week just for being my gunner. Not like Phoenix either. I mean, I wanna see you eat and crush other niggas that try and rival my crew, of course. You fuck wit' me and I'll get you filthy rich."

Kool Aid rubbed his chin. "I ain't got the patience for that hustling shit. I like upping my pole on a nigga and stripping his ass. Fast money at its finest. If it's your word that you gon' keep me fed, then it's my word that I'ma fuck wit' you on some other shit. We locked in." He bumped guns with me to seal our pact.

"Bet then, nigga. So I'ma need for you to knock off as many of his spots as you can to hit his pockets. The more broke he becomes, the faster we can emerge as the new kings of Memphis. You just do you though, and I'll make the rest of the shit happen."

"Say less, cuz. It's time to get it as snakes, so we can rise as bosses. That's the goon way. We know this, and our fathers knew this too. It's all in our blood. Roll me to the crib, I'm so fucked up that I can't even thank straight. I gotta sleep some of this shit off so I can be on the move tonight. Both of these addresses going down."

"Bet those." I put my foot on the gas with a smile on my face, I had some shit up my sleeve that was about to catapult me to where I needed to be.

***

After helping Kool Aid get into the bed so he could sleep some of his high off, I made my way back out of his crib. Saleyah was on the porch waiting for me when I got back outside. She kept looking back at her house as if she was afraid that something bad was going to happen. I jumped and almost pulled my gun because she spooked me at first.

She grabbed my arm. "JaMichael, you remember that you said you'd help me if I ever needed you?" she whispered.

"Yeah, what's up?" I tucked my gun into the small of my back and pulled my Supreme shirt back over it.

She bit into her bottom lip. "Well, I'm kinda trying to get out of the house tonight. I just wanna chill with my girl for a few hours. My mother'll let me leave out as long as she knows that I'ma be with you. Maybe you can tell her that you're going to introduce me to your children. I mean, Bubbie has been over here a few times, but she has never brought the kids." She looked back at the house again.

I checked the time on my Patek. It was just after six-thirty, and I really didn't have nothing urgent to do. I looked Saleyah up and down. She had on a pair of blue jean shorts that were hugging her frame. Her thick thighs were on full display. They were well oiled and juicy. "How old are you, Saleyah?"

"Eighteen. I just turned eighteen a few weeks back. Why?"

I nodded. "Aw, nothing, I guess I was just wondering why a grown woman still gotta ask her mother if she can go out and spend some time with her girlfriend. Yo' moms be trippin on you like that?"

She placed her finger against her lips. "Shhh, boy, she got ears like a hawk." She pulled me down to my truck and we got inside. She waited until the door was closed before she started again. "My mother is not like other guardians. She feels that since I am still living under her roof and eating her food and on her Obamacare while I am in college that I am basically still a little kid. She knows how messed up Memphis is, so she's just a little bit overprotective. But it's not really her that I'm worried about." She glanced back to the house again.

"If you ain't worried about her, then who are you worried about?"

"Kool Aid. He thinks that he runs the house. I mean, he does because he provides a lot for all of us, but he's not our father. No matter how much he thinks that he is." She sighed and crossed her arms.

There was just a hint of light coming off of the street. It illuminated the interiors of the truck. My eyes went down and drank in those juicy thighs on her young ass. "Awright, so what time are you supposed to be meeting your girlfriend?"

"In an hour. We just wanna chill at her house - in her room, of course - for a bit, and then I can come back home, and all should be well."

"Yo' li'l ass hot, that's all that is." I laughed.

She blushed. "So? It's not like I'm not human. I mean, everybody has needs. I am no different. So are you going to help me get out of this hell hole tonight?" She grabbed a hold of my right arm and sort of hugged it. I could feel the heat coming off of the soft skin in between her titties.

"Yeah, I got you. Let me go in here for a second so I can talk to her. This what you're wearing?" I asked, hoping that it was. I didn't mind seeing her parade around in her li'l outfit for a few hours.

"Oh heck no. I gotta go get dressed. You get the go ahead, and I'll meet you back down here in about twenty minutes." She opened the door and proceeded to call her mother by title.

***

I knocked on the door to Jody's bedroom and expected for her to tell me to hold on a second, then she would come outside into the hallway. Instead, she cleared her throat and told me to come inside. So I turned the knob and opened the door. "Jody, I wanted to holler at you about Saleyah. I was gon' let her chill wit' me and her li'l cousins for a few hours. Then bring her back at about ten o'clock."

Jody was 5'5" tall, light-skinned, with green eyes. She weighed about 145 with short, naturally curled hair. She stood up from the bed in a pair of pink boy shorts that were all up in her crack. She wore a tight white T-shirt that showcased the fact that she wasn't wearing a bra on her double D breasts. "Boy, close the door, you're letting all the heat out."

My eyes were bugged out of my head, but I followed her directives. I closed the door and turned back to her. Damn, she was smoking. "Damn, Aunty, you sho' I ain't caught you at a bad time?"

She laughed. "Nawl, come here." She motioned with her finger for me to come to her.

I walked up to her and stood in her face. She took her two little hands and held my face. She eyed me closely. "Damn, boy, you look so much like Taurus that it's almost scary." She rubbed her thumbs across my eyebrows, and then then down my face again. "Back in the day, your father had a way of breaking women down. They say he was a savage on every level. You anythang like him?"

This was my first time ever meeting Jody in person. Prior to this we had only talked on the phone, or by Zoom. "I mean, I don't know. I never got a chance to really be around my father like that. He was locked up before I started to walk."

"Well, that's terrible, because you would have loved him, I suppose." She ran her hand over my chest.

I smiled. "Well anyway, I wanted to let you know that I was taking Saleyah out with me tonight, and I'll have her back by ten."

"Oh no you ain't. I already know how you Stevens get down. Saleyah is your little cousin. If I let her go out of this house with you tonight, she definitely ain't coming back a virgin." She laughed. "Am I lying?"

I frowned and made it seem like I was offended, when I knew damn well I was about to find a way to fuck Saleyah's li'l ass. Her girlfriend too, if I had anything to say about it. "Nawl, it ain't even like that. It's my job to protect her. That sick stuff didn't even cross my mind, but I gotta be honest, standing here and looking at you in all of this glory, that crosses my mind with you. Damn, you so fine, my uncle had to be killing dis body."

She laughed. "Boy, I'm old enough to be your mother." She waved me off and looked away.

She just didn't know that I was the wrong nigga to play that mommy game with. I have had mommy issues my whole life. I felt that older women were the sexiest women on earth, and for me, there was nothing more alluring than an attentive, nurturing mother. That shit was my weakness. Out of nowhere, I grabbed her to me and cuffed her ass.

She yelped and bucked her eyes. "What are you doing?"

"The same thang my daddy should of did behind Juice's back if had the chance to hit this ass." I tossed her onto the bed and rushed her.

Ghost

Chapter 16

Jody didn't act like she wasn't with everything. As soon as I tossed her on the bed, she laid back and spaced her thick thighs. I reached between them and ripped her panties off of her as hard and as fast as I could. She moaned and pulled her top over her head. She was braless.

I rushed to get my Gucci belt unfastened. As soon as it was, I dropped my pants. My pistol fell on the carpet, and I ignored it. I dropped my boxers and snatched her ass closer to me. "I'm 'bout to fuck Juice's baby mother? Ain't life a bitch."

She shivered. "Come here, 'cause we gotta hurry up." She pulled me closer by my arm. She took a hold of my piece and stroked it up and down before she sucked me into her mouth. In a matter of seconds, her face was bobbing up and down in my lap. She stopped, spit on the head, and stroked me some more. Then she took me deep into her throat, gagging and fucking like a pro.

I slapped her on the ass and squeezed that yellow booty. Just knowing that Kool Aid was only a few rooms over sleeping while I was getting head from his mama made me feel dirty on the one hand, and like a boss on the other. This was something that niggas never heard of happening before, and it was some real life shit.

Jody popped me out of her mouth and stood up before she bent over the bed. "Hurry up. That overbearing-ass boy ain't let me have a boyfriend in over a year. I swear he thinks that I am his woman. I need some dick so bad. Hurry up and put it in, JaMichael. Please."

She ain't need to beg. I found the crease between her sex lips and pushed forward. Her heat started to consume me inch by inch. I grabbed her waist and pulled her backward as hard as I could. Smack! Her ass had collided in my lap loudly.

"Mmm." She took the pillow off of the bed and bit into it. She pushed back into me over and over again while I fucked her as hard and as fast as I could with no mercy. "Mmm. Mmm. Mmm. Mmm. Mmm-mmm!" she hollered into the pillow.

I was focused. I was fucking Kool Aid's mother. That's what was driving me forward. With every thrust, I was imagining his bitch ass coming at, Bubbie while I was on lock and this was me getting my revenge. I sped up the pace and rolled my finger around her ass hole after sucking the digit into my mouth. She stopped for a second so she could feel it better. I sunk it all the way in, and pulled it back out, just to do it again.

"Yes, that's what I want. Fuck me right there, JaMichael, just like yo' daddy did. Please." She leaned forward on her knees and opened the drawer next to her bed. She grabbed a small bottle of oil, and squirted it in between her cheeks. "Right here. It's been so long."

I massaged it into her back door and started to finger that ass again. She whimpered. "Uhhhh. Uhhhh, you gotta hurry up. That boy doesn't ever sleep too long. Fuck me."

I put her on her knees and got behind her. As soon as I did, I lined myself up and sank into her rosebud. She opened her mouth wide and stuffed her face into the pillow. Once I got to fucking her with all of my might, her moans turned into loud groans. She slammed back on me, harder and harder, clapping into my waist.

I closed my eyes and imagined Kool Aid's face walking in and seeing me fucking his mama in the ass, and I couldn't help laughing. I clenched my teeth and slowly opened my eyes, fucking her so fast and hard that I felt my cum swimming to the top of the surface. "I'm finna cum in dis ass, shawty. I'm finna cum in my aunty ass. Aww shit."

Bam. Bam. Bam. Bam.

She bounced back into me over and over and over. She threw her head back and grabbed the pillow. She screamed into it and crashed back into me five more times really hard. Then she was cumming. I could feel her anal muscles gripping me.

That sent me off. I pulled my piece out of her ass and jerked it until I was bussing all over her back, and thighs. I laid my dick in the middle of her crack and rubbed it around her ring while I nutted all over her booty.

***

"So how in the hell did you get my mother to agree to let me come out with you until eleven o'clock? You must've worked your magic, huh?" Saleyah asked while she sipped out of the lemonade concoction that I'd mixed: Percocets, Mollie, and a little codeine inside of. It was a mixture that we in Memphis called Feelings, 'cause that's what it got you in after about thirty minutes of consumption.

"Girl, it doesn't matter how he made it happen. At least we get to be out here with our cousin for a few hours," Sia chimed in. "I mean, it sucks that Tamara couldn't get off of work, but at least we still get to chill." Sia and Saleyah were identical twins, but Sia had a bit more weight on her. She was what I liked to refer to as Memphis thick: strapped in all the right places with a li'l gut. A real sista from the south. She held up the bottle of Feelings that I had given her. "Dang, this lemonade got me feeling some type of way. I mean everythang tingles. Saleyah, let me sit up front with him. You ain't doing nothing but just sitting there."

We were parked at the top of Center Hill overlooking the city of Memphis. The hill was a popular hangout for high school kids to go and have make out sessions, at least from what I remember. The scent of both Sia's and Saleyah's perfume had me hard as a rock. I was finding it hard to contain myself.

"What do you expect me to do? Damn," Saleyah returned.

"I'ma show you, if you move." Sia climbed her thick ass into the front of the truck and sat right in the console. She got on her knees and placed her hand on my thigh. "JaMichael, I'm smart enough to know that you ain't tryna kick it with two females on a Friday night unless you tryna fuck. I know who we might be to you and all dat, but let's just be real. We don't really know each other like that, and I ain't ashamed to tell you that I thank you fine as hell. My mama and our brother don't let us do anything. What do you say 'bout letting me get some of dat pipe befo' we gotta go back in the house?"

"Sia!" Saleyah called.

"What? I'm just cutting to the chase. He sitting here all fine and shit. I ain't got time to play that demure virgin role, and you're just as horny as me. That's why you were trying to hit up Tamara. I'm tired of listening to you finger yourself every night. You always riling me up. Don't understand why you acting all scared and stuff. JaMichael, from the street, he gets what dis thang is, don't you, JaMichael?" She squeezed my thigh and smiled up at me biting, on her bottom lip.

Saleyah waited for my response. She sat there and blushed. She bit on her loose nail and squeezed her thighs together tightly. When our eyes met, she lowered hers.

Five minutes later, I had Sia, sitting on the hood of my truck with her thighs wide open. She was faced toward the city, and I had my back to it. I placed a knee on the bumper of my Benz truck and moved her G string to the side. Her pussy popped out, shaven and plump as a balled fist. She opened her thighs further. I sniffed up and down her gap, then opened her up so I could see her pink. Even in the light of the moon, it shone as if it had a light of its own.

Saleyah stood on the side of us. "Dang, y'all out here all in the open. What if somebody drives up and catches you two?" she asked, appearing to be nervous.

"Girl, you are too high strung. If you ain't trying to be a part of the get down, then why don't you go and wait in the truck for us?" Sia said this as she felt me kissing up and down her pretty pussy.

"Fine then, I will." She stomped her foot and went back into the truck.

I licked up and down Sia's pussy, sliding a finger in and out of her gap. She humped forward into the digit with her head thrown back. We were just getting started and already she was oozing as if water was coming out of her gap. I slurped that shit up and slipped another finger into her. That sent her mad.

"Unh! Unh! Unh! JaMichael! Damn, cuz." She jumped faster and faster. Her tongue played on the side of her mouth. Before I could get into my mode, with the whole fingering thing, she pushed me away, and jumped off of the hood. She bent over the bumper just like her mother had bent over the bed less than an hour ago. "Come on, Ghost." She shivered. "Damn, I forgot that was your name, it drives me crazy. Mmm. But come on, cuz, hurry up and fuck me before we gotta go back into the house."

"Y'all better get from out there. Damn, we gon' get in trouble," Saleyah whined.

"Girl, be quiet! Shit! Come on, JaMichael." She slammed the side of her ass cheek. Smack!

I got behind her and felt up and down her crease. Her lips were already wet with her dew and dripping. I slipped my finger all around her groove until it slipped inside of her hole. Then I removed it and slipped into her after a little wiggling from side to side. Her heat attacked me right away.

She threw her head back and looked me in the eyes. "Fuck me, cuz!"

I pulled her all the way on my dick by taking a hold of her waist. I knew I didn't have much time, so I had to handle my business quickly. I fucked her hard and fast. Our skins slapped loudly in the night. Over and over again. She tried her best to make her pussy muscles grip me, but I was hitting that shit so hard that all she could do was whimper.

"Aww. Aww. Aww. JaMichael! I'm so sorry. Unh! Unh! Please! Please. Unh! Unh! Unh! Sia hollered. She held on to the bumper of the truck, taking her dicking.

I slapped that ass hard. "Fucking this li'l fresh pussy. I'ma fuck dis pussy whenever I want to. Ain't I?" I smacked that ass two times hard.

"Uhhhhhh! Shit!" She lowered her head and pushed back on me ten quick times. She threw her face to the sky, and screamed at the top of her lungs, before she came. "Uhhhh! Uhhhh! Big cuz! Oooooh shit, I love you! I love you."

I turned her around and picked her up. She wrapped her legs around me. I slipped back into her and fucked her up against the side of the truck while Saleyah snuck her hand into her panties and played with her pussy while I tossed her sister up and down in front of her. It was crazy because even though I was fucking the shit out of Sia, my eyes were pinned on her twin. The sight of watching her doing what she was doing got to driving me crazy. When she pulled her pink bikini cut panties all the way down to her knees, I couldn't take it no more. I came deep in Sia, bouncing her ass up and down.

Sia screamed and came again and licked the side of my face. "I love you. I love you. Aww fuck, I do."

I lowered her to her feet with my piece leaking from her juices. I shot past her and rushed into the truck, catching Saleyah off guard. Before she could make a move or say anything. I got between her slimmer thighs and rubbed all over her box. At first her panties were in the way, but after pulling them down and throwing them on the floor of the truck I had complete access to what I wanted. She had my whole truck smelling like strawberry-scented pussy.

"What are you doing, cuz? I like girls." Saleyah started.

"Don't listen to her, Ghost. She doesn't know what she is missing, that's all," Sia said, climbing into the passenger's seat, still rubbing between her thighs.

I wasn't trying to hear that shit no way. I rubbed her pussy slowly and meticulously. She was dripping. I sucked on her neck. "Come on, baby cuz, first time for everythang. Let me get some of this shit. Just a one-time thing." My finger slipped into her hole.

"No, I like girls." She closed her eyes and opened her thighs a bit wider.

"I know you do, and that's cool." I lined myself up and slowly pushed.

"No, stop." Saleyah placed her hands on my chest and pushed me slightly.

I slipped into her tight fit and I felt like I was being suffocated. There was barely enough room to get inside. I was about three inches in. "Damn, what's good wit' this?" I tried to push a little harder.

She arched her back and tried to get away. "Wait, it hurts." She pushed at me.

"It's her first time, Ghost." Sia hurried over to us. And pulled me back from, Saleyah. "Here, let me do this first." She pushed Saleyah's knees upward and covered her pussy with her mouth.

"Unh! Unh! Unh! Sia, why?" She grabbed the back of her head and rode her face for five minute. Then she screamed loudly and fell backward, shaking like crazy.

"Okay, come on." Sia motioned for me to come over to her.

I climbed back between Saleyah's thighs, and slipped right in now that she was dripping. She fought me for a second, but after a few minutes, I was fucking her at full speed. While she screamed her head off, that only encouraged me to fuck faster and harder.

"JaMichael! JaMichael! Cuz! Cuz! Oh my fuckin' cuz!" She arched her back and hollered that she couldn't breathe. Then she started to shake uncontrollably.

I sucked her breasts through her blouse. Sia yanked it up, exposing her titties. I took her nipples one at a time, fucking the shit out of her. When I came, I curled her into a ball and bussed deep in her womb. She, like her sister, swore up and down that she loved me.

When I dropped them back off that night, they both smelled a way. They both kissed my lips and walked into the house on wobbly legs. After smashing Saleyah, Sia insisted that I hit her again, so I did. Then I hit Saleyah again, then I was out of stamina. As I drove away, I couldn't help but to feel like a straight boss. In one night I had smashed Kool Aid's mother and both of his sisters. I broke up laughing.

Chapter 17

Four days later, Phoenix invited me out to a club that he was thinking about purchasing, saying that he wanted to talk to me about some business. So even though I was going to talk to him and not to party, I still got fresh in black and red Gucci from head to toe with the matching red bottom LeBrons. I had five hundred thousand dollars' worth of jeweler around my neck, and an iced Richard Mille around my left wrist.

When we stepped into the club it was packed. We were ushered to the back by a thick-ass redbone bottle girl that had her blond hair in Shirley Temples. She had a thong that sliced her cheeks just perfectly, and she walked on bowed legs. Every now and then she would turn around and smile at us as she guided us through a packed dance floor.

When we went to the VIP section, there were three bottles of champagne on the table. All were sitting on ice. I grabbed the Ace of Spades and popped the cork, drinking right from the bottle. "So what brings me out here, Phoenix? I know you don't need me to be here to scout this bitch wit' you. It ain't like it's about to be mine or nothing like that." I laughed and took another sip from the bottle of champagne.

Phoenix, popped the cork on the Moët. "I'm down eighty G's in two nights, Mane. Ma'fucka done had the nerve to knock off three of my spots within hours of each other. That's eighty G's in cash, and a hundred G's in product. I'm starting to thank that a ma'fucka don't take me seriously." He drank from the bottle again.

I placed my bottle on the table. "So that's why you got me out here? You thanking that you 'bout to press me to find out what's going on or something?" I was curious.

He shook his head. "Nawl, far from that. I'm thanking that since you said you were gonna' be on top of this whole thang that you would have been. Instead, it looks like I'm taking more L's than anything else. Which is funny, 'cause I don't take letters my nigga. I take lives."

Now I was frowning. "Wait a minute, mane. What you trying to imply?"

"Ain't implying shit. Dis how dis finna work li'l cuz, I'ma give you a day to get to the bottom of dis whole thang for me. You said that you was gon' be able to crack the case, so that's what you gon' do. If you don't, I'm sorry, but you gon' have to accept the consequences."

Now I was fuming. "Say, bruh, I ain't never been scared of no pistol play. You finna talk shit to diarrhea, then let's get it. How the fuck you wanna do this?" I stood up.

Phoenix pulled his phone out and slid it across the table. "I ain't got no time to be playing wit' you, JaMichael. I'm 'bout my paper, shawty. Take a gander at dat right there."

I picked up the phone and saw my three children sitting on a couch with duct tape around their shoulders, and mouths. Some big nigga held Jahmya with a Coronavirus mask across his face the read Duffel Bag Cartel across it. He mugged the camera before the screen went black.

"Yo, so that's what this coming to?" I asked, feeling my heart beat out of my chest.

"Yeah, mane. I'm starting to get the inkling that you might know more than what you letting on. Each house that was hit you knew about. So you gon' either cough up my scratch and give me the ma'fucka or ma'fuckas that's doing this, or... Nawl ain't no or. We too far gone." He sucked his teeth.

"So this what we finna do? Those yo li'l cousins, and this is what you do."

"Bitch, I'm Duffel Bag. Fuck blood if it's getting in the way of my paper. You got twelve hours to bring me my money and the culprit that's doing this shit. Time is ticking, so if I was you, I'd make it happen. Oh, and keep your eyes on that red door right down that hall." He flung the phone in my lap and stood up, leaving the club.

I sat there for a moment with my mind racing. I noticed that I'd seen my children and not Bubbie. Where the fuck was she? My head got to spinning like crazy. Just as I got up ready to call her with my own phone, I saw her walk out of the back door - the same door that Phoenix had told me to keep my eyes on. Bagg walked beside her with his right arm around her neck. The sight of them together, and the thought of what Phoenix had done to my seeds, was enough to send me over the deep end. I ducked low out of VIP after grabbing the phone and my pistol from the seat.

***

"Stop! Stop! JaMichael! What are you doing? What are you doing to him? Stop!" Bubbie hollered with her hands covering her mouth.

"Bitch, stop saying my ma'fuckin' name!" I snapped and flung her toward the open passenger's door of Bagg's red Lamborghini. She fell on the seat. I had a black ski mask over my head and had spent the last thirty seconds pistol whipping the shit out of him. You'd think that a nigga that was worth millions would have top notch security, but I guess that wasn't the case.

Bagg looked up at me from the concrete with blood running down his forehead and face. He was already beginning to swell up. "What the fuck you want from me, homeboy? If it's money, it's ten G's in my pockets, and another twenty under my driver's seat? Dis shit light." He wiped the blood away and struggled to breathe through his nose, which was turned awkwardly.

"Get yo' ass up and come wit' me." I yanked him up by his Gucci sweater and led him down the parking lot after telling Bubbie to recover the money that he had just jacked about having. She cursed me out, asking what the fuck was I doing, but then she followed my commands and did what I told her to anyway.

When we got to the little Lexus trapper I had been rolling around in for a few days, I popped the trunk and forced him to get on his knees. He slowly did and appeared woozy and weak from his blood lost. "Bubbie, get yo' ass over here and tie his hands with that duct tape right there. Hurry up!"

She ran over. "I swear to God I hate you. I hate you with everything that I am as a woman. You just don't want me to be happy!" she screamed.

"Bitch, shut up and do what the fuck I said!" I snapped.

She ran over and once again, followed my commands. "I don't understand this."

"Bitch, you can quit playing like you ain't set me up. Dis is Memphis. I knew what it was when you kept that pussy on the shelf. My ego just wouldn't let me believe I couldn't smash a bitch wit' three kids. It's good though."

"Bagg, I swear to God, I didn't have nothing to do with this. I would never have even thought about some bullshit like this. You have been so kind to me," Bubbie swore.

"Mane, fuck all dat bullshit lying, shawty. Just do what ya man said so he don't take me life," Bagg ordered. "Y'all fucked up, I get it. It is what it is."

"But Bagg, I swear…" Bubbie started with a long piece of tape on her finger.

I busted Bagg in the mouth and slammed the tape across it. "Shut yo' bitch ass up. And bitch, you get in the car. I can see you feel a way 'bout dis when he told you all he was tryna do was fuck. Simple ass. Hurry up." I picked Bagg up and stuffed him in the trunk, slamming it closed. Then I hurried and jumped in the Lexus before pulling off out of the parking lot with murder on my mind.

Ghost

Chapter 18

"He got my babies. He got my babies. He got my babies. Why would he have my babies?" Bubbie said this over and over again while she paced back and forth in front of me.

I had Bagg laid in his side, duct taped and bleeding. We were at his mansion out in Nashville, and I was just finishing up stuffing the last duffel bag with cash. There were three in all. I didn't know how much I had hit his bitch ass for, but it was a lot. I stood up after zipping the last bag and looked down on him. I pulled the .40 Glock from my waist. "What you gon' say to stop me from knocking yo' noodles out, nigga?" I'd already removed the tape from his mouth.

"Before I jumped in the rap game, I was on that stick-up shit too. I know how dis shit go. I can take this loss. All I ask is that you don't kill me. I got my whole career ahead of me, and I ain't never been one to fuck wit' Twelve. Dis shit'll stay right hurr. No retaliation, no cops, no media, no nothing. On my shawties, mane, it'll be like it never happened. Dis gets to the press, my album sales drop. Dat's a fact," Bagg assured me.

"You sayin' worse comes to worst, you can leave dis shit in the street? Huh, nigga, that's yo' word?" I asked, ready to smoke him.

"Yeah, mane. You ain't gotta kill me. Just like you got yo' book thang, I got my music. I know you only doing this shit 'cause a ma'fucka done took yo' babies for ransom. Dis Memphis, bruh. It comes wit' the game. I can accept dis. Dat's on everythang. Don't kill me."

I stood over him for a long time, finding it hard not to do so. I knew that he had an army of niggas behind him, and that whenever he broke free they would be at me, so the smartest move was to kill him. But then, on the flip side, he was a young dope boy turned music entrepreneur from Memphis. He had, in a sense, made it out. Who was I to take his life, and in a sense wind up giving him the fate that his people, his family, and even himself thought that he avoided? I couldn't do that. "Say mane, I ain't gon' kill you. You got a bright future. The world loves that trap music. Just gon' say dat if you ever seek retribution, bring that shit to me only. Keep it in the streets. Bubbie ain't know shit 'bout dis. Dat's my word."

He nodded. "Dis shit dead right hurr. On my mama."

"Yeah, awright. Come on, shawty. I ain't gon' kill the nigga."

For the first time after hitting a major lick, I allowed for the nigga to live. I knew it would come back to haunt me, but I couldn't take Bagg's life. The world should thank us for not doing so, straight up.

***

Kool Aid hopped into my Benz truck later that night high as a kite. He was scratching and smacking his lips. He took a sip from the bottled water from my console without asking me. He burped and laid his head back on the seat. "Say mane, dat nigga Phoenix holler at you?" he asked, looking over at me with his eyes barely opened.

I pulled from in front of his house and curled the right side of my upper lip. "Yeah, that nigga freaking out 'bout his traps getting hit. Say he feels like ma'fuckas thank he sweet or something. He say somethin' to you?"

Kool Aid nodded his head. "Nigga came and snatched up my mama and both my sisters. Say if he doesn't find out who been knocking his shit off and get his money back dat he gon' kill my people. I fucked up. I ain't got that money no more, and I can't admit that it was me, JaMichael. What I'ma do?" He drank from the bottle again and pulled his nose.

"Nigga, you been knocking his shit back on a weekly basis. You mean to tell me that you ain't got his money stashed nowhere, and you ain't got none of his dope?" I became heated.

He shook his head. "Nawl, mane. See what had happened was, a few months back when I was on my kick door shit…" He paused, and drank from my water bottle again. I watched his Adam's apple move up and down before I grabbed the bottle of water from him and threw it out of the window. "Fuck you do that for?"

"Say mane, nigga, get to it."

"Awright. A couple months back, I robbed this one trap house that I didn't know belonged to the Sinaloas. They found out that I did and in exchange for my life, they told me all I would have to do was to knock off Phoenix's spots and give the money back to them. Which is crazy because the same Sinaloas that Phoenix is copping from is the same ones that got me hitting his traps. But I don't know, mane. All dis shit is becoming too much for me, cuz. I feel like I'm in too deep. Ma'fucka got my head spinning like crazy." He closed his eyes for a minute. Then he opened them and pulled out a Visine bottle. He twisted the cap and snorted the dripping mixture.

I allowed for him to toot five more drips. I pulled my phone out and held it up so I could see Phoenix's face on the screen. "You heard that, cuz?" I asked him. Kool Aid's eyes were still closed.

"Yeah, nigga, I heard it. Make that nigga pay for his sins," Phoenix ordered.

"Say no mo'," I returned, pulling my gun from under the seat.

"What?" Kool Aid opened his eyes.

I placed the .40 Glock to his cheek. "Money over blood, nigga."

Boom!

The bullet knocked a massive hole through his face. Blood went everywhere. He punched me and somehow opened the car door, falling to the rail of the railroad tracks we were parked beside. He got up running with plasma leaking out of his mug. I chased him and waited for him to fall. I held the phone to make sure that Phoenix could see him clearly in the camera. Then I stood over him and pulled the trigger four times, blowing his face off. He lay still, leaking.

"Dat good enough for you?" I asked, looking into the camera.

"That's done, nigga, get out of there." The screen went black.

"Bitch-ass nigga." I took one final glance at Kool Aid's body before I jogged to the truck and pulled off.

***

Phoenix came and dropped two duffel bags filled with cash beside me three days later as I sat in my living room after just waking up. I don't know why Bubbie had let him into the house while I was sleeping, but I was definitely gon' get on her ass when he left.

He stood up. "Look, li'l cuz, that shit was just bidness. I wasn't gon' never hurt my li'l cousins, but I had to make it look like I was so that you would respond like you did. However, don't take that shit personal. You already know how dis game go. But there go your money. A deal is a deal."

There was no way that I was going to accept what he'd done to my children and myself. I had to have his life, but I was going to wait until the right moment. For now, he was lacing me with my cash - the same cash I was gon' use to crush the Duffel Bag Cartel and help my Heartless Goons to rise again. "It's all good, cuz. It was just business."

"Yeah, keep that sentiment. Well, I'ma gon' get up out of here and fuck wit' you at another time. I know you and your family are still picking up the pieces. Once again, it was just business." He nodded his head and eyed the cash. "Spend that wisely. Them Bread Gang niggas already talking revenge. It's a must you invest in security just like I am. Peace." He left out of the front door, followed by two of his bodyguards, before he got in his Phantom and pulled off of the block.

I stood up breathing hard. I had to have that nigga's life. I had to crush his mob. I couldn't take this bitch feeling he had me enduring. The Duffel Bag Cartel had to be smashed, and Phoenix right along with them.

I took a deep breath and knelt before my bags of money. A slight smile spread across my face. I unzipped the bag and grabbed out a stack of hundreds, nodding, when I felt a metal pole come to the back of my head. The shotgun cocked.

"Yeah, bitch-ass nigga, seems like I got out at the right time, didn't I? You remember me?"

I felt a sharp kick to my back. I fell to my stomach and rolled over and looked into the menacing eyes of Rock. He still had on his prison blues. Fuck, how did I forget about him? "Shit."

"Shit is right. On my mama, yo' bitch ass deserves dis." He aimed and...

To Be Continued...
Heartless Goon 6
Coming Soon

Submission Guideline

Submit the first three chapters of your completed manuscript to ldpsubmissions@gmail.com, subject line: Your book's title. The manuscript must be in a .doc file and sent as an attachment. Document should be in Times New Roman, double spaced and in size 12 font. Also, provide your synopsis and full contact information. If sending multiple submissions, they must each be in a separate email.

Have a story but no way to send it electronically? You can still submit to LDP/Ca$h Presents. Send in the first three chapters, written or typed, of your completed manuscript to:

LDP: Submissions Dept
Po Box 944
Stockbridge, Ga 30281

DO NOT send original manuscript. Must be a duplicate.

Provide your synopsis and a cover letter containing your full contact information.

Thanks for considering LDP and Ca$h Presents.

<u>Coming Soon from Lock Down Publications/Ca$h Presents</u>

BOW DOWN TO MY GANGSTA

By **Ca$h**

TORN BETWEEN TWO

By **Coffee**

THE STREETS STAINED MY SOUL **II**

By **Marcellus Allen**

BLOOD OF A BOSS **VI**

SHADOWS OF THE GAME II

By **Askari**

LOYAL TO THE GAME **IV**

By **T.J. & Jelissa**

IF LOVING YOU IS WRONG... **III**

By **Jelissa**

TRUE SAVAGE **VIII**

MIDNIGHT CARTEL III

DOPE BOY MAGIC IV

CITY OF KINGZ II

By **Chris Green**

BLAST FOR ME **III**

A SAVAGE DOPEBOY III

CUTTHROAT MAFIA III

DUFFLE BAG CARTEL VI

HEARTLESS GOON VI

By **Ghost**

A HUSTLER'S DECEIT III

KILL ZONE **II**

BAE BELONGS TO ME III

A DOPE BOY'S QUEEN III

By **Aryanna**

COKE KINGS V

KING OF THE TRAP II

By **T.J. Edwards**

GORILLAZ IN THE BAY V

3X KRAZY III

De'Kari

THE STREETS ARE CALLING II

Duquie Wilson

KINGPIN KILLAZ IV

STREET KINGS III

PAID IN BLOOD III

CARTEL KILLAZ IV

DOPE GODS III

Hood Rich

SINS OF A HUSTLA II

ASAD

KINGZ OF THE GAME VI

Playa Ray

SLAUGHTER GANG IV

RUTHLESS HEART IV

By Willie Slaughter

THE HEART OF A SAVAGE III

By Jibril Williams

FUK SHYT II

By Blakk Diamond

TRAP QUEEN

By Troublesome

YAYO V

GHOST MOB II

Stilloan Robinson

KINGPIN DREAMS III

By Paper Boi Rari

CREAM II

By Yolanda Moore

SON OF A DOPE FIEND III

By Renta

FOREVER GANGSTA II

GLOCKS ON SATIN SHEETS III

By Adrian Dulan

LOYALTY AIN'T PROMISED III

By Keith Williams

THE PRICE YOU PAY FOR LOVE II

By Destiny Skai

I'M NOTHING WITHOUT HIS LOVE II

SINS OF A THUG II

By Monet Dragun

LIFE OF A SAVAGE IV

MURDA SEASON IV

GANGLAND CARTEL III

CHI'RAQ GANGSTAS III

Ghost

By **Romell Tukes**
QUIET MONEY IV
EXTENDED CLIP II
By **Trai'Quan**
THE STREETS MADE ME III
By **Larry D. Wright**
IF YOU CROSS ME ONCE II
ANGEL III
By **Anthony Fields**
FRIEND OR FOE III
By **Mimi**
SAVAGE STORMS III
By **Meesha**
BLOOD ON THE MONEY III
By J-Blunt
THE STREETS WILL NEVER CLOSE II
By K'ajji
NIGHTMARES OF A HUSTLA III
By King Dream
THE WIFEY I USED TO BE II
By Nicole Goosby
IN THE ARM OF HIS BOSS
By Jamila
MONEY, MURDER & MEMORIES II
Malik D. Rice
CONCRETE KILLAZ II
By Kingpen

HARD AND RUTHLESS II

By Von Wiley Hall

LEVELS TO THIS SHYT II

By Ah'Million

Available Now

RESTRAINING ORDER **I & II**

By **CA$H & Coffee**

LOVE KNOWS NO BOUNDARIES **I II & III**

By **Coffee**

RAISED AS A GOON I, II, III & IV

BRED BY THE SLUMS I, II, III

BLAST FOR ME I & II

ROTTEN TO THE CORE I II III

A BRONX TALE I, II, III

DUFFLE BAG CARTEL I II III IV V

HEARTLESS GOON I II III IV V

A SAVAGE DOPEBOY I II

DRUG LORDS I II III

CUTTHROAT MAFIA I II

By **Ghost**

LAY IT DOWN **I & II**

LAST OF A DYING BREED I II

BLOOD STAINS OF A SHOTTA I & II III

By **Jamaica**

LOYAL TO THE GAME I II III

Ghost

LIFE OF SIN I, II III
By **TJ & Jelissa**
BLOODY COMMAS I & II
SKI MASK CARTEL I II & III
KING OF NEW YORK I II,III IV V
RISE TO POWER I II III
COKE KINGS I II III IV
BORN HEARTLESS I II III IV
KING OF THE TRAP
By **T.J. Edwards**
IF LOVING HIM IS WRONG…I & II
LOVE ME EVEN WHEN IT HURTS I II III
By **Jelissa**
WHEN THE STREETS CLAP BACK I & II III
THE HEART OF A SAVAGE I II
By **Jibril Williams**
A DISTINGUISHED THUG STOLE MY HEART I II & III
LOVE SHOULDN'T HURT I II III IV
RENEGADE BOYS I II III IV
PAID IN KARMA I II III
SAVAGE STORMS I II
By **Meesha**
A GANGSTER'S CODE I &, II III
A GANGSTER'S SYN I II III
THE SAVAGE LIFE I II III
CHAINED TO THE STREETS I II III
BLOOD ON THE MONEY I II

By **J-Blunt**
PUSH IT TO THE LIMIT
By **Bre' Hayes**
BLOOD OF A BOSS **I, II, III, IV, V**
SHADOWS OF THE GAME
By **Askari**
THE STREETS BLEED MURDER **I, II & III**
THE HEART OF A GANGSTA I II& III
By **Jerry Jackson**
CUM FOR ME I II III IV V VI
An **LDP Erotica Collaboration**
BRIDE OF A HUSTLA **I II & II**
THE FETTI GIRLS **I, II& III**
CORRUPTED BY A GANGSTA I, II III, IV
BLINDED BY HIS LOVE
THE PRICE YOU PAY FOR LOVE
DOPE GIRL MAGIC I II III
By **Destiny Skai**
WHEN A GOOD GIRL GOES BAD
By **Adrienne**
THE COST OF LOYALTY I II III
By Kweli
A GANGSTER'S REVENGE **I II III & IV**
THE BOSS MAN'S DAUGHTERS I II III IV V
A SAVAGE LOVE **I & II**
BAE BELONGS TO ME I II
A HUSTLER'S DECEIT I, II, III

WHAT BAD BITCHES DO I, II, III
SOUL OF A MONSTER I II III
KILL ZONE
A DOPE BOY'S QUEEN I II
By **Aryanna**
A KINGPIN'S AMBITON
A KINGPIN'S AMBITION **II**
I MURDER FOR THE DOUGH
By **Ambitious**
TRUE SAVAGE I II III IV V VI VII
DOPE BOY MAGIC I, II, III
MIDNIGHT CARTEL I II
CITY OF KINGZ
By **Chris Green**
A DOPEBOY'S PRAYER
By **Eddie "Wolf" Lee**
THE KING CARTEL **I, II & III**
By **Frank Gresham**
THESE NIGGAS AIN'T LOYAL **I, II & III**
By **Nikki Tee**
GANGSTA SHYT **I II &III**
By **CATO**
THE ULTIMATE BETRAYAL
By **Phoenix**
BOSS'N UP **I , II & III**
By **Royal Nicole**
I LOVE YOU TO DEATH

By Destiny J
I RIDE FOR MY HITTA
I STILL RIDE FOR MY HITTA
By **Misty Holt**
LOVE & CHASIN' PAPER
By **Qay Crockett**
TO DIE IN VAIN
SINS OF A HUSTLA
By **ASAD**
BROOKLYN HUSTLAZ
By **Boogsy Morina**
BROOKLYN ON LOCK I & II
By **Sonovia**
GANGSTA CITY
By **Teddy Duke**
A DRUG KING AND HIS DIAMOND I & II III
A DOPEMAN'S RICHES
HER MAN, MINE'S TOO I, II
CASH MONEY HO'S
THE WIFEY I USED TO BE
By Nicole Goosby
TRAPHOUSE KING **I II & III**
KINGPIN KILLAZ I II III
STREET KINGS I II
PAID IN BLOOD **I II**
CARTEL KILLAZ I II III
DOPE GODS I II

Ghost

By **Hood Rich**

LIPSTICK KILLAH **I, II, III**

CRIME OF PASSION I II & III

FRIEND OR FOE I II

By **Mimi**

STEADY MOBBN' **I, II, III**

THE STREETS STAINED MY SOUL

By **Marcellus Allen**

WHO SHOT YA **I, II, III**

SON OF A DOPE FIEND I II

Renta

GORILLAZ IN THE BAY **I II III IV**

TEARS OF A GANGSTA I II

3X KRAZY I II

DE'KARI

TRIGGADALE I II III

Elijah R. Freeman

GOD BLESS THE TRAPPERS I, II, III

THESE SCANDALOUS STREETS I, II, III

FEAR MY GANGSTA I, II, III IV, V

THESE STREETS DON'T LOVE NOBODY I, II

BURY ME A G I, II, III, IV, V

A GANGSTA'S EMPIRE I, II, III, IV

THE DOPEMAN'S BODYGAURD I II

THE REALEST KILLAZ I II III

Tranay Adams

THE STREETS ARE CALLING

Duquie Wilson
MARRIED TO A BOSS... I II III
By Destiny Skai & Chris Green
KINGZ OF THE GAME I II III IV V
Playa Ray
SLAUGHTER GANG I II III
RUTHLESS HEART I II III
By Willie Slaughter
FUK SHYT
By Blakk Diamond
DON'T F#CK WITH MY HEART I II
By Linnea
ADDICTED TO THE DRAMA I II III
IN THE ARM OF HIS BOSS II
By Jamila
YAYO I II III IV
A SHOOTER'S AMBITION I II
By S. Allen
TRAP GOD I II III
By Troublesome
FOREVER GANGSTA
GLOCKS ON SATIN SHEETS I II
By Adrian Dulan
TOE TAGZ I II III
LEVELS TO THIS SHYT
By Ah'Million
KINGPIN DREAMS I II

Ghost

By Paper Boi Rari
CONFESSIONS OF A GANGSTA I II III
By Nicholas Lock
I'M NOTHING WITHOUT HIS LOVE
SINS OF A THUG
By Monet Dragun
CAUGHT UP IN THE LIFE I II III
By Robert Baptiste
NEW TO MONEY, MURDER & MEMORIES
THE GAME I II III
By **Malik D. Rice**
LIFE OF A SAVAGE I II III
A GANGSTA'S QUR'AN I II III
MURDA SEASON I II III
GANGLAND CARTEL I II
CHI'RAQ GANGSTAS I II
By **Romell Tukes**
LOYALTY AIN'T PROMISED I II
By Keith Williams
QUIET MONEY I II III
THUG LIFE I II
EXTENDED CLIP
By **Trai'Quan**
THE STREETS MADE ME I II
By **Larry D. Wright**
THE ULTIMATE SACRIFICE I, II, III, IV, V, VI
KHADIFI

IF YOU CROSS ME ONCE

ANGEL I II

By **Anthony Fields**

THE LIFE OF A HOOD STAR

By Ca$h & Rashia Wilson

THE STREETS WILL NEVER CLOSE

By K'ajji

CREAM

By Yolanda Moore

NIGHTMARES OF A HUSTLA I II

By King Dream

CONCRETE KILLAZ

By Kingpen

HARD AND RUTHLESS

By Von Wiley Hall

GHOST MOB II

Stilloan Robinson

BOOKS BY LDP'S CEO, CA$H

TRUST IN NO MAN

TRUST IN NO MAN 2

TRUST IN NO MAN 3

BONDED BY BLOOD

SHORTY GOT A THUG

THUGS CRY

THUGS CRY 2

THUGS CRY 3

TRUST NO BITCH

TRUST NO BITCH 2

TRUST NO BITCH 3

TIL MY CASKET DROPS

RESTRAINING ORDER

RESTRAINING ORDER 2

IN LOVE WITH A CONVICT

LIFE OF A HOOD STAR

Heartless Goon 5

www.ingramcontent.com/pod-product-compliance
Lightning Source LLC
Chambersburg PA
CBHW060419260626
47161CB00005B/1701